'Well – you seem to have a pretty classic case of retrograde amnesia.'

The words felt like spiders crawling up my arms. 'What's that?' I whispered.

'Simply put, it's when you lose your memory of who you are. Sometimes you lose other things too, like things you've learned in school, and that seems to have affected you to a certain extent – you don't know who the Prime Minister is, for instance, but you still know your basic numbers and how to read. Plus you've probably retained things like how to tie your shoelaces, use a knife and fork, and so on.'

She smiled at me, like I should be just so overjoyed that I could still tie my shoelaces. I wiped my eyes, wanting to stab her. 'But – but I don't know anything about who *I* am?'

'No, that's what retrograde amnesia means.'

'So am I going to stay this way?'

Dr Perrin patted my hand. I bet they taught her that in med school.

'It's hard to say,' she said. 'This sort of amnesia is normally caused by some sort of trauma, which might be the car accident in your case. It's usually temporary, though I've heard of cases where it isn't. You'll probably start to regain some of your memories over time.'

'Probably. Great.'

ALSO BY LEE WEATHERLY:

CHILD X
MISSING ABBY
BREAKFAST AT SADIE'S

www.leeweatherly.com

Kat got your Tongue

Lee Weatherly

CORGI BOOKS

KAT GOT YOUR TONGUE
A CORGI BOOK 978 0 552 55197 7

First published in Great Britain by David Fickling Books,
a division of Random House Children's Books
A Random House Group Company

David Fickling Books edition published 2006
Corgi edition published 2007

1 3 5 7 9 10 8 6 4 2

The Random House Group Limited makes every effort to ensure that the
papers used in its books are made from trees that have been legally sourced
from well-managed and credibly certified forests. Our paper procurement
policy can be found at: www.randomhouse.co.uk/paper.htm

Typeset in New Baskerville by Falcon Oast Graphic Art Ltd.

Corgi Books are published by Random House Children's Books,
61–63 Uxbridge Road, London W5 5SA

www.**kidsatrandomhouse**.co.uk
www.rbooks.co.uk

Addresses for companies within The Random House Group Limited can be
found at: www.randomhouse.co.uk/offices.htm

THE RANDOM HOUSE GROUP Limited Reg. No. 954009

A CIP catalogue record for this book is available from the British Library.

Printed in the UK by CPI Bookmarque, Croydon, CR0 4TD

For Jean and Alan,
my wonderful in-laws

Much love to you both

Chapter One

Kat

The only thing I remember about it is this massive *bang*, but it didn't hurt or anything. It was more like a noise, or maybe just a sensation – I can't explain it. But then I was flying through the air, really flying, like a bird. I wasn't scared. It was great, in fact. I remember thinking, How cool, I could do this forever.

Then everything went black. Total cliché, but that's what it did, just like someone had flipped the lights off. When I opened my eyes again, I was lying in the middle of the road. I could see blue sky and clouds, and a ring of anxious faces staring down.

I blinked, gazing up at them. I wanted to ask someone what had happened, but it was as if I had forgotten how to talk. The asphalt felt hard and knobbly under my head, digging into my scalp. Woozily, I tried to sit up. About a dozen hands reached out and pushed me down at once.

'No, no, dear!' gasped a woman with a round face and glasses. 'Just lie there and rest.'

'That's right. The ambulance will be here shortly,' said someone else.

Panic kicked my stomach. Ambulance? Hang on, I'm fine! Even as I thought it, part of me knew it wasn't true. My head hurt, and so did my shoulder (quite a bit, in fact) – but I definitely *wanted* to be fine, so that I could get up and get away from these people. They were scaring me.

I pushed the hands away and managed to sit up. Not a good idea. The world dipped sideways and went fuzzy for a moment. I touched my spinning head, and my hand came away red and sticky.

It felt like snow had slithered down my spine. I started to shake as I gazed down at my red-stained hand, thinking, There's been some mistake. That can't be blood! But what else? Could it be ketchup, maybe?

It didn't look like ketchup.

The woman with the round face clutched my arm. I turned towards her in what felt like slow motion. 'Please, just lie down!' she said shrilly. 'You're hurt, you shouldn't be moving about!'

'OK, OK,' I murmured. Hands flew out from all directions, supporting me as I sank back to the ground. It was a relief, to be honest.

A siren wailed in the distance, coming closer. Wincing, I turned my head and saw a group of girls in school uniforms, huddled on the side of the road with tears running down their faces. I have to be dreaming this, I thought dazedly. Why were they crying when they didn't even know me? A short girl with ginger plaits stood staring at me, her face paper-white. I watched a dark-haired girl put an arm around her and whisper something in her ear.

The woman with the round face sank onto the kerb beside me, holding her head in her hands. 'I didn't even see her!' she moaned. 'She just ran out in front of me – there was nothing I could do—' Her voice choked to a halt.

Another woman gripped her shoulder. 'Don't worry, I saw the whole thing if you need a witness. She ran straight out in front of you, against the lights. If you ask me—' Her voice lowered abruptly. I was sure I heard the word *drugs.*

I swallowed. Was I on drugs? Was that why everything seemed so strange?

A screech of brakes, and then a door slammed. The crowd drew back as a man and woman in green jumpsuits knelt down beside me.

'Hi, I'm Sue,' said the woman. She had a fresh, scrubbed face, and blonde hair pulled back in a ponytail. 'Wow, you've got yourself a bit banged-up, haven't you? What's your name?'

I started to tell her, and then stopped. Because where there should have been a name, there was nothing at all.

Just – nothing.

I licked my lips as fear rocked through me. 'I – I'm not sure.'

'Not sure?' Sue frowned, and then she must have seen the terror in my eyes, because she patted my shoulder. 'OK, well, don't worry about it for now. Steady – here we go. Grab the other side, Craig.'

She and the man moved me onto a stretcher, and

then Sue nodded at the group of girls. 'Do any of you know her name?'

They looked sideways at each other, not moving. The black-haired girl still had her arm around the ginger one.

'Well?' said Sue. 'Come on, do you know her or not?'

A girl with loose blonde curls cleared her throat. 'She's called Kathy Tyler.'

Kathy Tyler? I stared up at her, feeling dazed.

'What year is she in?' asked Craig, doing up the final snap on the stretcher.

The blonde girl hesitated, glancing at the others. 'Year Nine,' she said finally. Her face was pale. 'Will – will she be all right?'

Sue didn't answer her. 'The school will have her contact details,' she said to Craig. 'Come on, let's get going.'

On the way to hospital, Sue gently cleaned my face up (I tried not to notice how the cloth came away bright red), took my pulse, shone a tiny light in my eyes. The siren blared around us, sucking up all the sound from everything else.

Kathy Tyler, I kept thinking. *Kathy Tyler.*

It sounded utterly bland, like someone in a cheesy movie – the American cheerleader who gets eaten by the monster. It didn't feel like it had anything to do with me at all. Had those girls really known me, or had they just made it up?

I groaned as Sue put a bandage on my forehead.

Everything hurt. My shoulder felt like someone was stabbing it.

'What happened, do you know?' asked Sue. There was a whispery noise as she tore a bit of adhesive strip off a roll. 'That car must have thrown you a good few metres.'

I thought of flying through the air again, and felt sick.

'I don't know,' I said. 'This woman said I just ran out in front of her, but – but I don't know why I'd do that.' I gripped the edge of the blanket they had draped over me, clutching it tightly. 'Do you think I'm on drugs?'

Sue taped the bandage down, her fingers firm and gentle. 'I don't think so, but they'll do tests when we get to the hospital, just to make sure.'

I licked my lips. They tasted salty. 'But – then why can't I remember anything?'

She frowned, glancing at my forehead. 'It might just be the shock.'

I swallowed, and Sue squeezed my hand. 'Don't worry. Craig's radioed ahead to the hospital to phone the school, so your mum should be there soon.'

My mum? It felt like I was tumbling, falling. I screwed my eyes shut, suddenly too scared to talk.

I didn't know who my mum was.

When we got to the hospital, Sue and Craig lifted me out of the ambulance. Like magic, the stretcher turned into a trolley-thing, with silver wheels clicking out from underneath it.

'Right, here we go,' said Sue, steering me into the building.

I kept craning my neck, peering around – hoping like mad that I'd see a woman, know she was *Mum,* and then everything would come flooding back to me.

A nurse with frizzy brown hair rushed up to us as we got inside, and she and Craig went into a huddle. I turned my head, straining to catch their conversation. '. . . stepped out into traffic and was hit by a car . . . head wound's minor, but she says she doesn't remember anything . . .'

Sue patted my arm. 'You'll be fine,' she said, and then suddenly she and Craig were gone, and I was being whisked off by the nurse.

'Right, let's get you sorted,' she said cheerfully, wheeling me down a long corridor. I swallowed hard, trying not to cry. I felt so alone, like I was the only person in the world. Which was stupid, since I was completely surrounded by people – doctors and nurses streamed down the corridor like busy ants.

'Is my mum here?' I asked.

'Sorry?' The nurse leaned her head close to mine without missing a step.

'My *mum,* is she here?' I said louder.

'Oh. I don't think so, not yet. You'll see her soon.'

The nurse took me into an examining room, and she and a doctor poked and prodded at me for ages. First they examined my head, and then they stitched up the gash in my forehead – it took four stitches, and hurt like anything, even though they gave me a jab first. All the while, they kept asking me questions: What school did I go to? What was my mum's name?

I don't know, I don't know, I kept saying. I felt so stupid, and the fear was like a dark cave swallowing me up. What was wrong with me? They were questions anyone should know. Finally they asked me to breathe into a tube thing, and to wee into a plastic cup.

'Do you want me to help you?' asked the nurse, and my cheeks caught fire.

'No, thanks.'

I almost wished I had said yes when I went into the bathroom. My head swam, and I had to grab hold of the disabled railing on the wall to catch my balance. I used the loo quickly, trying to hold the plastic cup so that nothing spilled. But my shoulder hurt and I couldn't hold the cup straight, so of course it did spill, and I thought I might throw up.

Afterwards, I washed my hands about a dozen times, using frothy pink soap from a dispenser on the wall. As the warm water played over my fingers, I glanced in the mirror – and froze.

I had never seen the girl looking back at me before.

She had wide green eyes, and wavy brown hair that came down to her shoulders. Her chin was pointed like a cat's. Actually, her whole face looked sort of cat-like – slanty cheekbones and a small nose. Faint freckles scattered across her nose and cheeks, and a blood-stained bandage blazed across her forehead.

I stared at her. She was wearing the same black uniform that the group of girls had been wearing. Desperately, I tried to find a memory that went back further than an hour ago. Something, *anything. Think!* I shouted at myself. Come on, remember!

But there was just a black hole. I didn't know this girl. I didn't know the first thing about her.

The nurse rapped on the door. 'Are you OK in there?'

I quickly dragged my eyes away from the mirror, feeling almost guilty. 'Yes, sorry.'

An hour or so later, I sat on a different examining table in a paper gown, trying not to shiver. My shoulder had a massive bruise on it from where I had landed, but it was just strained, as it turned out.

'It'll be stiff for a while, that's all,' said the doctor. It was another doctor, not the one who had stitched up my forehead. This one was old and paunchy, with a bushy grey beard and bristling eyebrows. 'You'll need to exercise it. Every day. *Don't* let it stiffen up.'

'Um – OK.' I started to chew a fingernail, and then stopped as I realized that I hardly had any fingernails left to chew. The girl in the mirror – Kathy Tyler – hadn't left me any.

The doctor frowned as he held a large slide up to the light. They had put me in this machine they called an MRI – a giant cylinder that took pictures of my brain. It was like being swallowed up by a humming, pulsing alien.

'Now then' – he put the slide down and gave me a hard look – 'about your head injury—'

He broke off as a nurse stuck her head round the door. 'Doctor, Miss Yates is here.'

His eyebrows drew together. 'Miss Yates?'

'Kathy's mum.'

I swallowed hard. Suddenly my throat felt two sizes too small. *Miss Yates,* when I was *Tyler.* What did that mean? Was she divorced from my dad – whoever he was? Had she remarried? *Who was she?*

'Oh, of course.' The doctor glanced at me. 'I'll be back in a minute; we just need to let your mother know what's going on.'

I managed a nod, and he left the room. I clenched the sides of the examining table. It felt like I'd spin away into space if I didn't hang on. Oh, *please* let it be OK, I thought. Please let my mum make everything all right. And yes, maybe that was a babyish thing to wish for, but I seriously didn't care at that point.

A few minutes later the door opened again, and the doctor came back. There was a slim dark-haired woman with him. She had the same pointed chin I had seen in the mirror, but her nose was longer, and she didn't have freckles.

She rushed straight over to me. 'Kathy! Sweetie, are you all right?' She started to give me a hug, and then stopped, pulling back anxiously. 'Wait, is this your bad arm? Oh, you poor love – what *happened*?'

I stared at her, taking in her face. Mum. This was my mum. But it was like *Kathy Tyler.* It didn't feel as if she had anything to do with me.

'Kathy?' said the woman. She frowned, touching my hair. 'Kathy, what's wrong?'

I swallowed, and shook my head. I couldn't speak.

She looked at the doctor, worry etched across her face. 'You said she was confused. What's wrong with her?'

He picked up the slide from the MRI again, holding it to the light. 'Well, we don't really know. Her drug test was clear, so even though there's no obvious sign of trauma to the skull, we did an MRI scan, which came out fine as well. That gash on her forehead looks a lot worse than it is – it's only shallow.'

My heart thudded against my ribs. 'Then why can't I remember anything?' I burst out.

The doctor's bald patch shone in the harsh light as he squinted at me. 'Well . . . maybe you can tell us. Is anything bothering you at school? A problem with your friends, maybe?'

Friends. Another black hole. I remembered the girls beside the road. Were they my friends? They hadn't acted like it.

'I don't know,' I said, hugging my elbow to my side. 'I don't remember anything about school, or – or anything.'

The woman – my mother – took my hand, leaning towards me. 'But, Kathy, you remember me, don't you?'

I shook my head. I couldn't look at her. 'No.'

'You . . . don't remember me?' Her brown eyes widened as she gripped my hand, and suddenly I knew that she couldn't do anything at all to make it better. I had been such a stupid baby to even hope she could.

Trying not to cry, I pulled my hand away. Her fingernails were digging into my skin, and it hurt. She pressed her hand to her mouth.

'Kathy, you don't—'

'*No!* No. I don't.'

Silence. I could feel her staring at me, her mouth loose and pleading. I glared down at my feet, feeling awful. But I *didn't* know her. What was I supposed to say?

The doctor glanced at the scan again. 'Well, we'll keep you here for a day or two, just for observation,' he said grudgingly. 'And meanwhile, a psychiatrist will have a little chat with you.'

His voice turned falsely jolly with that last bit, like, *Ho-ho, you're just so going to enjoy this.*

Great, I thought as tears swam up into my eyes. Now I was mad, on top of having a black hole for a memory.

The children's ward had stars on the ceiling and Rupert the Bear wallpaper, which just made everything slightly worse, somehow. The nurse handed me a cotton gown instead of the paper one. 'Here, I'll help you change,' she said.

Flames flew up my cheeks. 'I can do it.'

The nurse smiled. 'Well, obviously you *usually* can, but you might find it difficult just now, with your shoulder so stiff.'

I hesitated, because of course she was right. Maybe

my shoulder was only strained, but it felt like an anvil had been dropped on it. I could hardly move my left arm.

'I'll help you,' offered my mother softly. She stood to one side with her arms crossed over her chest, hugging herself.

Our eyes met, and I looked quickly away.

'No, um – that's OK, she can help.' I motioned to the nurse, and let out a breath when she rattled the curtain shut around the bed, closing my mother out. I couldn't help it. I knew *logically* that this was my mum, but it felt like some stranger off the street had offered to help me change. At least with the nurse, it was her job.

After the nurse had left, my mother sat beside my bed, trying to smile. 'Do you want the curtain open or closed?'

'Closed.' Part of me wanted it open – I could hear a TV going somewhere in the ward – but I couldn't bear the thought of talking to anyone. What if someone asked what was wrong with me?

My mother sat perched on the edge of her seat. 'I'm sure this is just temporary.' She fiddled with a silver ring on her finger. 'The doctor thinks it might be the shock of the accident, or – or something like that.'

I nodded, looking down at my hands. The nails really were in awful shape. Kathy hadn't just bitten them all off, she had picked at the hangnails until they were ragged and raw.

No, correction: *I* had picked at them. Me.

My mother kept smiling nervously, pushing her short dark hair back with one hand. 'It's so lucky that you weren't really badly hurt – that car must have been going quite fast when it hit you.'

'What happened?' I asked. 'How did it hit me?'

She shook her head. 'I spoke to the woman driving the car, and she doesn't know; you just ran out in front of her. She thinks maybe you were trying to cross against the light.'

'Oh,' I said. Crossing against the light? Had I really been that stupid?

My mother brushed my hair back with cool fingers. 'The important thing is that you're OK.' She tried to smile. 'You'll get your memory back soon.'

I took in her face. There couldn't be a mistake – she was obviously convinced that she was my mother, and so was everyone else. But I just didn't *feel* it. I didn't feel anything for her.

I cleared my throat. 'Um . . . listen. I don't – I don't know anything about myself. Or you. Could you—?'

The curtain around the bed swept open. A plump middle-aged woman with bright honey-coloured hair stood there, beaming at us. 'Hello, I'm Doctor Perrin. I'm here to talk to Kathy.'

'Oh.' My mother looked at me. 'Should I leave?'

Dr Perrin smiled, showing all her teeth. 'Yes, if you don't mind. We'll probably be about an hour or so.'

My mother stood up. Her hands hung helplessly at her sides. 'Well, I suppose I'll pop home for a bit, then, and come back around two.'

Home. 'Where are we?' I asked, fingering the edge of the sheet. 'What town, I mean?'

She glanced at Dr Perrin, who nodded. 'We're in Basingstoke,' she said. 'Hampshire.'

'Oh.' I sort of thought I had heard of them, but they were just names, really. Nothing to do with me.

My mother touched my arm. 'We'll talk later,' she whispered.

After my mother left, Dr Perrin plonked herself into the empty seat. 'Right! Do you know what a psychiatrist is?'

'Yes,' I said shortly. I wanted to tell her that maybe I didn't know who I was, but I wasn't stupid.

'Oh, good. Well, I just need to ask you some questions, all right?' She settled back in the chair, crossing her chubby legs. Picking up a pen, she held it poised over a clipboard. 'Can you tell me your name?'

I told her, and she nodded. 'And did you know your name when you first regained consciousness?'

'No.'

'Can you tell me what year it is?'

Another black hole. I pressed my lips together, trying to think. 'Um . . . 2004?'

I knew it was wrong, but she didn't comment. Her pen scratched on the paper. 'How old are you, do you know?'

I swallowed. 'I think – well, I think I'm probably a teenager, but I don't know how old, exactly.'

A hundred other questions followed, on and on.

Did I know my address? My middle name, if I had one? Who was the Prime Minister? What was sixteen divided by two? Some of the questions I knew straight off – like sixteen divided by two; that was easy – but most of them I didn't.

There was a pause as Dr Perrin scribbled down something else. I stared up at the stars on the ceiling. They had turned all watery. Out in the ward, some sort of kids' programme was on the TV. I could hear a little girl singing along to a song about rainbows, and someone else crying. I knew how they felt.

Finally Dr Perrin snapped the cap onto her pen and started to stand up. 'Right, I think that's all for now, Kathy.'

I sat straight up, ignoring the jabbing pain in my shoulder. 'But what's *wrong* with me?'

She hesitated, and then settled back into her seat again. 'Well – you seem to have a pretty classic case of retrograde amnesia.'

The words felt like spiders crawling up my arms. 'What's that?' I whispered.

'Simply put, it's when you lose your memory of who you are. Sometimes you lose other things too, like things you've learned in school, and that seems to have affected you to a certain extent – you don't know who the Prime Minister is, for instance, but you still know your basic numbers and how to read. Plus you've probably retained things like how to tie your shoelaces, use a knife and fork, and so on.'

She smiled at me, like I should be just so overjoyed that I could still tie my shoelaces. I wiped my eyes, wanting to stab her. 'But – but I don't know anything about who *I* am?'

'No, that's what retrograde amnesia means.'

'So am I going to stay this way?'

Dr Perrin patted my hand. I bet they taught her that in med school.

'It's hard to say,' she said. 'This sort of amnesia is normally caused by some sort of trauma, which might be the car accident in your case. It's usually temporary, though I've heard of cases where it isn't. You'll probably start to regain some of your memories over time.'

Probably. Great.

I lay curled up in my bed with the curtain drawn, listening to the TV. My cheeks were wet again: hot, stupid tears kept leaking out of my eyes. I swiped my hand across my face. I wasn't *sad*, I just – didn't feel very good.

I didn't feel good at all, in fact.

Out in the ward, it sounded like someone had grabbed a channel changer and was going berserk with it: *Rebel soldiers are thought to have . . . 'Tell us, when you found out about your wife, what—?' . . . And NOW, for a limited time only . . .*

And then the voices stopped, and the most amazing music floated past. I can't even describe it. It sounded rich, and grand, like – like the ocean pounding against the shore, or like galloping through a forest on a wild horse. I shut my eyes, my muscles relaxing as it carried me away.

'Not *that*! Are you barking?' called someone, and the channel changed again. Cartoon voices filled the ward.

I sat up in bed, leaning over and scraping the curtain open. 'Put it back!' I said.

A half-dozen startled faces looked at me. 'Back where?' said the girl in the next bed. She looked about my age, with blonde hair. Her leg was up in traction, and she had the channel changer in her hand.

My cheeks burned. I felt beyond stupid, but I had to say it anyway. 'Back to the music.'

She wrinkled her nose. '*That?* I only put it on to torture the kiddies.' But she clicked a button on the channel changer, and suddenly the TV on the wall showed dozens of musicians sitting in a semicircle. A conductor stood before them, waving his hands about, and the music crashed and soared.

I sank back against my pillows, drinking it in. It didn't last very long, though. After about a minute, a little boy across the ward whined, 'Do we *have* to watch this?'

Instantly, about four other voices piped in with, 'Yeah, this sucks! Put the cartoon channel back on!'

The girl next to me shrugged. 'Troops are getting restless.'

'Fine, change it.' I tried to sound like I didn't care. When she clicked onto the cartoon channel, I closed the curtain and put a pillow over my head.

When my mother came back later that afternoon, there was a man with curly auburn hair and sideburns with her. He was *very* tall, and wore a blue jumper with dancing polar bears on it.

'Kathy, do you know who this is?' my mother asked, sitting down and pulling off her jacket. Her brown hair looked tousled from the wind, and the tip of her nose was red.

The man picked up another chair and carried it over. He winked at me as he closed the curtain around us. 'Get it right first time, and there's a prize.'

I almost laughed, even though nothing seemed very funny to me just at that moment. (I can't imagine why not.)

'Are you – are you my dad?' I asked. My heart beat faster. I really hoped he was. He had such a nice smile, and warm, friendly eyes.

'Nope.' The man dropped into the chair, raking his hair back with a grin. His legs looked like they went on forever in his faded jeans.

A sudden spot of red dotted my mother's cheeks, one on each side. 'No, he – oh, Kathy, I'm sorry; I should have explained. This is Richard, my partner. Your dad and I are – divorced.' The red deepened. She quickly looked down at her handbag, dropping her keys into it.

'Hi,' said Richard, and held out his hand to me. 'Pleased to meet you.' I shook his hand slowly, wondering who my dad was, in that case.

Before I could ask, my mother pulled something out of a white carrier bag. 'Look, we've brought this to show you – some photos from home. The doctor said anything that might help spark your memory would be a good idea.'

She put a small blue book on my lap and opened it up. 'This is you when you were three. Does it look familiar?'

I stared down at the photo. A little girl was sitting on a beach in a blue swimsuit, building a sandcastle. She had the same wavy dark hair I had seen in the mirror, and I guess the same green eyes as well, though I couldn't tell – her eyes were narrowed at her castle as though the sun were in them, or maybe like she was concentrating really hard.

I touched the edge of the photo, trying to take in the fact that this was me. A piece of my past from the black hole. But it was just a little girl named Kathy who I had never seen before.

'Was this in Basingstoke?' I said finally.

My mother glanced at me. 'No, Bournemouth . . . We used to live there. You loved the beach. We used to take picnics down there, and stay all day.'

I couldn't think of anything else to say. I knew I should have a thousand questions, but it just felt completely unreal. The girl in the photo could have been a cardboard cut-out.

Nobody was moving or saying anything, so finally I reached down and turned the page.

My mother craned her neck a bit as she looked down. 'That's your sixth birthday party – see, you got a stuffed panda. Remember? You called him Barney; you used to take him everywhere with you.'

The girl in the photo was taller now, wearing a party hat and hugging a black and white stuffed bear with a huge grin on her face. She had chocolate smeared across her mouth. A dozen other girls crowded around her, waving little plastic dolls at the camera.

'And Kathy, look. I brought Barney with me – see?'

My mother pulled a scruffy-looking bear from the carrier bag and put it in my arms. She sat back, smiling expectantly. Richard glanced at her, and put his hand on her knee.

I held Barney up, wanting so much to feel – *something*. But he was just a tatty old toy, grey and battered with age. His ears drooped, and he was missing one of his yellow eyes. Maybe I had thought Barney was fabulous when I was six, but I sure wouldn't be taking him everywhere with me now.

'Do you remember him?' asked my mother, leaning forward. Her eyes encouraged me.

I shook my head. 'Um – could I look at the next photo now?'

Her face fell. 'Oh . . . yes, of course.' She took Barney back from me, her fingers lingering on his head as she put him into the bag.

Richard winked, and I let out a breath and smiled at him. At least *he* didn't look like it was the end of the world if I didn't recognize a stuffed panda.

On the next page the girl was older again, maybe eight or nine. She stood on a stage playing a violin, wearing a blue dress. Bright lights shone on her face. Her knees were bent slightly, her dark eyebrows drawn together as she played.

I traced the photo with my fingers. 'I – do I play the violin?'

My mother nodded. 'You're *so* talented, Kathy. You know, you reached grade five when you were only ten.'

'What's that?'

'It's like a test,' said Richard. 'To show how much you know. Taking grade five when you're only ten means that you were a big girlie violin-swot, basically.'

Were? 'Don't I play any more?'

My mother sighed, and rubbed her cheek. 'Well, no. You haven't played in a couple of years.'

I stared at the photo. The girl looked so completely intent on what she was doing, so lost in her music. 'Why not?'

'I don't know. I guess . . . I guess you just lost interest.'

I could see tiny grey roots in my mother's hair as she gazed down at the photo. It was like she had gone back in time – back to when her daughter knew who she was, and played the violin like a big girlie swot.

My stomach tightened. I was starting to seriously hate these photos.

Finally my mother turned the page – and I caught my breath. There I was, wearing a black and white uniform and smiling straight at the camera. It was the same face I had seen in the mirror before. Exactly. The same light dusting of freckles, the same eyes and hair.

'That was taken before Christmas,' said my mother softly. 'About two months ago . . . It's just turned March!'

When I didn't say anything, she cleared her throat and added, 'You're in Year Nine.'

'How old does that make me?' I couldn't stop looking at the photo.

'Thirteen. You'll be fourteen in a few months.'

I stared down at the girl's flat, smiling face, wishing I could crawl into her head and know what she knew. But there was this mammoth wall around her, with barbed wire and KEEP OUT! THIS MEANS YOU! signs. I shut the album, not wanting to see any more.

Silence. My mother started to say something, and stopped, gazing down at her hands.

'Just give it time,' said Richard easily. 'You'll remember or you won't, that's all. We'll all get by either way, right, Beth?'

My mother nodded, her hair bouncing on her shoulders. 'Of course! Oh, of course, we didn't mean to – to pressure you. It was just, the doctor said . . .' She trailed off.

'Is that your first name – Beth?' I pushed myself upright against the pillows.

She tried to smile. 'Well, Elizabeth, but everyone calls me Beth.'

'Oh,' I said. I didn't say what I was thinking, which was that I wished *I* could call her Beth. 'Mum' was too weird. I didn't even know her.

'What's wrong with you?' asked the blonde girl in the next bed. She was wolfing her food down like she had been systematically starved ever since she got here.

I took a bite of rice, stalling for time. I was feeling totally stir-crazy after Beth and Richard left, so I had asked the nurse to leave my curtain open while I ate. Big mistake. I *knew* this would happen. Finally I swallowed, and pointed at my bandaged forehead. 'I fell.'

The girl's eyes widened. 'Oh, right. Do you have concussion or something?'

I shrugged, and looked at the TV on the wall. The sound was off, and it looked completely tedious – men in suits talking.

'What's your name, anyway?' asked the girl. 'I'm Sarah.'

'I'm, um—' I stopped. *Kathy* wouldn't come out. It just wouldn't; it didn't have anything to do with me. I looked down at my dinner, poking at the peas with my fork. 'I mean – well, I'm called Katherine, but—'

Sarah laughed. '*Katherine!* Oh, very proper. Does that explain why you like boring classical music, then?'

I stared at her, a flutter of excitement rustling in my chest. She was right. The rest of my past might still be in a black hole, but at least I knew *something* about me – I liked classical music. Maybe not all classical music, but I liked what I had heard that afternoon. So I wasn't a total black hole after all.

'What?' asked Sarah.

I smiled and looked down, keeping it to myself. 'No, I'm not called Katherine.'

'What, then? Kathy?'

I shook my head, and Sarah scraped the last of her custard from its plastic container, licking the spoon.

'You're going to make me guess, aren't you? OK, let me think. Kath? Katie? Kat?'

Kat. My shoulders relaxed. It felt right.

I grinned. 'Yeah, you finally got it. I'm called Kat.'

Chapter Two

Kathy

7 January
Today's M-day: moving-in day. I knew it was coming, obviously, but I still HATE IT!!! *Why* does he have to live here? Why can't they just date, the way they have been? I don't care if he stays over occasionally, I just don't want him to move in! This is OUR house, mine and Mum's, nothing to do with him!

The downstairs is complete chaos now – cardboard boxes everywhere, all over the dining table and the floor. There's even one on the fish tank! I just went down to get something to eat and literally stopped in my tracks; I hardly even recognized the place. Richard smiled at me as he came in the front door carrying still MORE boxes, and said, 'Oi, aren't you going to help, then?'

Not likely. I didn't say anything to him, I just kept going into the kitchen. Then I came back upstairs and banged my door shut, which Mum obviously didn't hear or else she would have been after me like a shot. I've got Robbie Williams blaring now, so that I don't have to listen to all the commotion going on, and can pretend that everything is the way it used to be.

Later
Mum just stuck her head in to tell me it was almost time for tea. I told her I wasn't hungry, and she looked really irritated and told me to be downstairs in ten minutes, because Richard had cooked a special moving-in tea for us all, to celebrate. Adults are so unbelievably dense sometimes that it's unreal. As if HIM moving in is anything for ME to celebrate!

9 January
Poppy and Jade came round after school today. I was so embarrassed for them to see the downstairs – it's still a tip with Richard's boxes everywhere. Then I was even more embarrassed, because Richard himself came out of the kitchen. I thought he was at work! But no, apparently he took the afternoon off to finish unpacking. Great. He said hi to us and then he started showing Poppy and Jade one of his cringe-worthy card tricks. I wanted to die, but Poppy and Jade were actually enjoying it. I FINALLY managed to drag them up to my room, and Jade said, 'Wow, he's so nice, you're really lucky.'

She just so didn't get it. Neither did Poppy. I tried to explain to them how I felt, but Poppy said that *her* mum's boyfriend was a total waster, and that I should be thankful, because it could have been much much worse. I said, 'Fine, but your mum's boyfriend doesn't live with you! It's completely different.'

Then Jade said, 'Ooh, maybe they'll get married

and have a big wedding! And you can be a bridesmaid!' She and Poppy started talking about dresses and what kind of flowers I should carry to go with my hair. I mean, PLEASE!!! I asked them to stop going on and on but they wouldn't, so finally I put a CD on and turned it right up to drown them out.

They took the hint and Poppy tried to change the subject, but then Jade got all stroppy and said I was being selfish, and that my mum was obviously really happy with Richard, so I should be happy for her. God! I'm not trying to stop Mum *seeing* him – I mean, who cares? He just shouldn't *live* here. He's not my dad, he's got no right!

But there was no way I could talk about Dad to them. Just no way. They don't have a clue about any of it, and anyway I don't like thinking about it very much. So I just laughed sarcastically and said, 'Oh yeah, I'm really thrilled that my mum's with some guy who looks like Elvis.'

Jade snapped something back and we went back and forth for a while, the two of us getting really arsey with each other, and Poppy trying to sort of moderate, the way she usually ends up doing. She was taking Jade's side more than mine, though. I could tell that she thought I was being unreasonable. They finally ended up stomping off, with Jade saying that I was being a total drama queen and should get over myself. That is so ironic coming from her, queen of the flounce.

I got out Cat after they left and cried for a bit. I couldn't help it. It's just SO UNFAIR that they're not even trying to understand how I feel! I mean, OK, maybe I haven't told them all the reasons why, about Dad and everything, but they should still try to understand and not just say I'm being selfish.

Later
Tea was a total nightmare. My eyes were red, and I could see Mum noticing, and of course Richard kept talking on and on, cracking his unfunny jokes and trying to get me to smile. *Why* can't he just leave me alone?? He had cooked lasagne, my favourite, but then he kept making this big deal over it, going on about his special secret ingredients and talking in a phoney Italian accent. I just ignored him. Afterwards, when Mum and I were doing the dishes, she said she knew this must be difficult for me, but that we'd all adjust with time. And meanwhile could I please try to be pleasant to Richard, because he really liked me.

I'm just so touched. I'm just so over the moon.

'We'll all adjust with time' – right, like it's really some hardship for her to adjust when it's what she wanted in the first place!

10 January
When I got to school this morning I saw Poppy and Jade walking a bit ahead of me, so I ran to catch up with them and said sorry to Jade, and she said sorry back. We've done this about a hundred times since we first became friends, so *that* was no big deal. But then I told them what I was thinking last night, that I thought they should try to understand how I felt. I said

it really nicely and reasonably, but it didn't make any difference. Jade just flipped her hair back and said, 'Oh no, not *that* again!'

Poppy told her to be quiet and said, 'Kathy, what's wrong? Why don't you like him?'

And I tried to explain, but all I could come out with was stuff like, 'It's our house, he shouldn't be there.' Jade was rolling her eyes around in no time, and even Poppy looked pretty unconvinced.

So I told them to never mind, they obviously didn't understand at all and there was no point in me trying to explain. Jade just laughed and said there was definitely no point if I didn't have any better reasons than what I had just told them. Then Poppy laughed too, and even though I had told myself that I would be very calm and not get upset, I thought I might start to cry. So I quickly walked ahead of them without saying a word. They let me go too. And they're supposed to be my friends.

We sort of made up again at lunch, but I wasn't talking much, because all I could think about was Richard, living in our house. Like he's supposed to be my father. I HATE it! I felt like crying, or screaming, or doing *something*, but I knew I couldn't because they wouldn't understand. So I didn't say anything. But then Jade said I was sulking, and I had to smile and say, 'No, I'm not. I'm just being quiet.'

It was a pretty terrible day, actually.

There was a new girl in our class today. She's called Tina McNutt, and she looked even more miserable than I felt. I'm not surprised with a surname like

McNutt, plus she has bright ginger plaits – ouch. Anyway, I feel really sorry for her, and not just because of the name and the hair. Starting a new school mid-term is the worst thing in the world.

11 January

Jade said that I'm no fun at all any more, and that I should stop sulking and get a life. I think Poppy agreed, even though she said, 'Oh, Jade,' and tried to look sympathetic.

Things are still completely wonderful here at home too. Mum's getting fed up with me, even though she pretends to be all understanding and patient. Well, she'll be waiting a long time for me to be happy about this.

Richard seems to have taken over all the cooking. He's moved loads of special pots and pans and spatulas and things into the kitchen, not to mention a huge wooden block filled with knives. He saw me looking at it and said, 'Don't worry, I never use them in anger.'

Please. He thinks he's so funny, but he's not. I told him I was just wondering where his apron was.

12 January

I don't believe it! Mrs Boucher called me into her office today and told me that she wants me to be Tina McNutt's FAB buddy. FAB stands for Friends and Buddies (apparently), and means that I have to walk her to all her classes and introduce her to all my friends. Normally I wouldn't mind, but I just *so* don't feel like it right now. I've seriously got enough on my mind as it is.

I sort of tried to say that to Mrs Boucher, telling her how much homework I have and all that, but she said, 'What does that have to do with showing Tina around and introducing her to your friends?' So I was stuck. Plus she said that she thought I'd be the perfect person, because I know what it's like to start a new school mid-term. Argh!

She's going to arrange a meeting for Tina and me tomorrow, in her office, so we can get to know each other. Great. Any other time, I might actually like doing this, but NOT NOW!!!

Anyway, now that I'm stuck with Tina, I was sort of watching her this afternoon. She's really short, with those awful ginger plaits I've already mentioned, and she has a crocheted handbag with a big purple flower on it – what a hippy! She has this perpetually worried expression on her face at the moment, but she looks like she might be a laugh if you got to know her.

Which I obviously am. It's so unfair, no one ever listens to you when you're my age.

Richard and Mum have gone out to see a film. They asked me if I wanted to go along, but I said no. As if I'd really want to tag along after the pair of them, with everyone thinking that Richard is my *father*. No, thank you! Not to mention having to listen to Richard's jokes all night, and the way Mum laughs after practically everything he says.

Like, before they left, Richard whipped her coat off the rack and held it out for her like she was a movie star or something. '*Mademoiselle*'s wrap,' he said, and then he gave me a wink. Ick. I tried not to notice the way he rubbed her arms after he helped her on with the coat.

I'm sitting downstairs now, with the TV all to myself for a change. Peace and quiet, hurrah!

13 January

I had the meeting with Tina and Mrs Boucher today. Tina's OK, I guess. We talked about where she's from (some little village in Shropshire I had never heard of), and the sort of stuff she likes to do. She plays the violin, she said. She's really into it. I mean, *seriously* into it – her eyes completely lit up when she talked about her lessons. She's just done her grade three, she said.

Hearing her go on about it made me feel sort of funny, so I just said, 'Oh, that's great,' and didn't say anything else. When she asked me what I like to do, I said I like to read and go swimming.

I'm supposed to meet her at the front gates on Monday, to start walking her to her classes and introducing her to everyone. I've already told her all about Poppy and Jade, and how they're my absolute best friends and have been ever since Mum and I moved here two years ago. I think maybe I was showing off a bit – wanting her to know what brilliant mates I have.

Later

Why does she have to play the *violin*?

Chapter Three

Kat

Beth and Richard's house was exactly like all the others in their neighbourhood – a brick terraced house on a crowded street. The windows had red and white trim, and their front garden had gravel on it, and a big pot with a spiky-looking plant.

'Oh, we're lucky . . . look, a parking space right here.' Beth angled the car into a space in front of the house, and gave me a quick, nervous smile. 'Sometimes we have to circle around for ages before we find a space. You do get good at parallel parking, living here.'

I had only stayed at the hospital for two days, and then they said I might as well go home, since having a sore shoulder and a cut on my forehead wasn't exactly life-threatening. But I should probably also keep seeing Dr Perrin, they said. Since I was so obviously completely nuts.

I swallowed, and pushed at the sleeve of my shirt. When they said I could go home, Beth had brought some fresh clothes to the hospital for me to wear – plain white knickers and a bra, along with a crisp pair of jeans and a patterned red and black top. They fit perfectly, even if I had never seen them before.

'Does it look familiar?' Beth was watching me, her eyes trying not to look worried. I realized that I had just been sitting there, staring up at the house.

I unfastened my seat belt, struggling a bit with my stiff shoulder. 'No, not really.' Not at all.

It was just the two of us. Richard was still at work. Beth worked from home – she did something called life-coaching, which meant that she gave people advice on how to live their lives.

Just then, she looked like *she* could use some advice.

Beth took a deep breath as she swung open the front door. 'Right, well, here we are. Home sweet home.' Pulling her jacket off, she hung it on a hook on the wall. She saw me hesitating, and motioned to a doorway on the right.

'That's the sitting room; it goes through to the dining room and kitchen. The bedrooms are upstairs, and—' She started laughing suddenly, pushing her dark fringe out of her eyes. 'Oh, this is too strange, giving you a guided tour!'

Well, it didn't seem strange to *me*; I had never seen the place before. I went to the doorway of the sitting room and peered into it. It had grey carpet that was just the tiniest bit worn, and an oversized blue sofa and chair. A piano stood in one corner, with photos clustered on top of it.

Beth trailed after me. 'Do you – I mean, does any of it look familiar?'

I shook my head, thinking, Stop *asking* me that!

'No, well . . . never mind. Let's have a cup of tea, what do you say?'

She led the way into the kitchen. It had bright cream-coloured walls. Down at one end was a table and chairs that sat in front of a bay window, looking out to the back garden.

Beth switched on a black plastic kettle. 'Would you get the cups, Kathy? Oh, sorry – I mean Kat.' She tried to smile. She hadn't exactly been thrilled when I told her I'd changed my name.

I glanced up at the rows of pale wooden cupboards, but of course it was no use. 'Um . . . I don't know where they are.'

'Oh! I'm sorry, I wasn't thinking – they're right here, behind you.' Beth forced a laugh as she opened one of the cupboards. 'See? This one's your favourite.' She placed a mug with yellow roses on it in front of me, turning it round so that the handle was at a perfect angle. The handle had roses on it too.

I didn't like it much, but it didn't seem worth arguing over. 'Which one's your favourite?' I asked. Since we were doing favourites.

She flapped an arm helplessly. 'Oh, any one . . . it doesn't matter.'

I chose one with tumbling clowns for her, and stood silently as Beth poured boiling water over the tea bags.

'Sugar?' She slid a sugar bowl across the worktop

towards me. I shook my head, stirring milk into my tea.

'But you always—' She bit the words back and managed a smile. 'Well! Shall we sit down? We, um – had the breakfast nook put in last year, so that we don't always have to sit in the dining room. We can just sit in here and look out at the garden.'

I glanced over at the yellow table and chairs, and imagined sitting there, trapped, trying to make conversation. 'Um . . . could I see my room?'

Beth put her mug down so quickly that a bit of tea sloshed over the rim. 'Oh! Yes, of course, of course you'd like to – to see where you'll be. Settle in, I mean. How thoughtless of me.' She seemed so flustered that guilt swamped over me.

'It's OK. I mean, I don't have to see it right now.'

'No, no, that's all right . . . Come on, it's this way.'

I followed Beth back through the house. The carpet was the same soft grey everywhere, like misty rain – on the stairs, down the first-floor corridor.

'This is your room,' said Beth, stopping in front of the last door on the right. 'Oh, and that's the loo there' – she pointed at a door down the hall – 'and that's my study, and our bedroom.'

I nodded, only bothering to take in where the loo was for now. I could figure the rest out later. Because I'd be here for a long time, wouldn't I? This was my home.

The thought brought a hot lump to my throat. I didn't know what to feel, and suddenly I was just desperate for her to go away. 'Thanks,' I managed.

'I'll, um – just take a nap or something, if that's OK. I mean, I'm pretty tired.'

Beth's face seemed to crumple. 'Oh, Kathy—' Suddenly she was hugging me, her arms wrapped tightly around me as a great, choking breath racked through her.

I stiffened. I couldn't help it. After a minute she pulled away, her eyes bright. 'Sorry. I didn't mean to . . . I'll just leave you here, shall I? I'll call you when it's time for tea.'

She left quickly, her footsteps hurrying down the stairs. Alone in the corridor, I swallowed and looked at the door. It had flower stickers on it. Part of me was dying of curiosity, and the other part just wanted to turn and run.

I opened my bedroom door and stood on the threshold, taking it in. It was so compact, like a cabin in a spaceship. There was a single bed with a plain white duvet, and Barney the stuffed panda lying draped across the pillow. A long shelf ran across the wall above the bed, groaning with books and CDs. On the opposite wall there was a desk with a computer, and a wardrobe. Loads of posters.

Just a few days ago, I had lived here. I had been Kathy. I had lain on that bed, and sat at that desk, and thought . . . what?

Edging into the room, I closed the door and leaned against it with my arms behind me. I gazed at the nearest poster, taking in brooding dark eyes and black hair. An actor, maybe?

Finally I got up the nerve to open the wardrobe.

There were a few black and white school uniforms, and then a bunch of other clothes. I was almost afraid to touch them. It was like the real Kathy was going to rush in and say, 'What are you doing? Get off my things!'

Gingerly, I scraped a few of the coat hangers down the rack, examining the different tops and skirts. Some of the clothes were OK – I saw a bright blue top that I liked – but mostly it looked like a thundercloud had exploded in the wardrobe. A black turtleneck with clinging sleeves. A brown miniskirt. A tight black T-shirt. It was totally and utterly depressing.

I reached the end and dropped my hand. Get used to it, I told myself. *You're* the one who chose them, even if you can't remember it any more. And somehow I doubt that Beth is going to buy you a whole new wardrobe.

I sighed and shut the wardrobe door. But then I didn't know what to do next. Hugging myself, I sank onto the floor, gazing around. The cut on my forehead ached. It was so quiet. It was spooky.

Finally I got up and went over to the desk. I had been hoping that maybe there'd be a school paper or something I had left out, but no, it was all clinically tidy. And somehow I couldn't bring myself to open one of the desk drawers. *Stupid*, I know, but I just couldn't. It felt like I was trespassing.

Instead, I turned round and looked at the books on the shelf. Lots of romances – that was a surprise. The CDs clicked against each other as I flicked through them. Nothing that looked even remotely like the ocean-crashing orchestra I had heard in hospital. I had played the violin, though! You'd think I'd have been into something apart from pop.

Apparently not. So I didn't know anything about the old me after all.

Grabbing a CD at random, I put it in the player, and almost got deafened by the blare of drums and guitars that pounded out of the speakers. I turned down the volume and pulled one of the romances from the shelf. Kicking off my trainers, I settled down on the bed, moving Barney aside.

As I opened the book, I thought wearily that there was one good thing about amnesia, at least – I wouldn't remember how the story ended.

I guess I fell asleep, because the next thing I knew it was dark, and the CD had stopped. The book lay on my chest. I yawned, stretching – and then I started, knocking the book to the floor with a muffled *bang*. Beth stood in the doorway of the bedroom, watching me with a raw expression on her face.

She sort of laughed when she saw that I was awake. 'Tea's ready.' She held an arm out to me as I slid off the bed, and then quickly dropped it again. 'Richard made your favourite,' she added hopefully.

I couldn't tell her that I had no idea what my favourite was. 'Great. I mean, thanks.'

Richard was already at the dining table when we got downstairs. I slid into the empty seat and he grinned at me.

'Enjoy your kip?'

I nodded and smiled shyly at him, feeling my muscles relax. Richard seemed so mellow, like he was happy if I remembered, and happy if I didn't. Thank God he was here, and I wasn't stuck alone with Beth!

My favourite meal was lasagne with garlic bread, as it turned out. It was really good, but I was too nervous to enjoy it. I looked down at my plate as I ate, incredibly conscious of the noise my fork was making.

Suddenly Beth leaned forward, smiling. 'Oh, Kat, I almost forgot to tell you – Nana and Jim want us to come round sometime soon.' She saw my blank expression and her shoulders wilted slightly, though she managed to keep smiling. 'They're your grand-parents,' she explained. 'My parents . . . They've got lots of photos and things to show you.'

'Oh.' Suddenly I didn't feel very hungry any more. I rested my fork on the side of my plate. Wonderful. More people I didn't know showing me photos and staring hopefully at me; I could hardly wait.

'Couldn't I see my dad instead?' I asked. I glanced at Richard, and then at Beth again. 'I mean – does he know I've lost my memory?'

Beth had been about to take a sip of wine, but now she hesitated, putting her glass down. 'Kathy, I – there's something I need to tell you.'

'Kat,' I whispered.

She shook her head impatiently. 'Kat. I – I didn't want to tell you this while you were in hospital, because . . .' She trailed off, looking at Richard.

'Beth was hoping that your memory would come back, and then you wouldn't need to be told,' said Richard. His eyes met mine, and he smiled sadly, swirling red wine about in his glass.

'Need to be told what?' I sat up straight in my seat, ignoring the throbbing of my sore shoulder.

Beth sighed. 'Kat, your father – your father passed away over two years ago.'

Passed away. I didn't understand what she meant at first; it sounded like something from a nursery rhyme. It took me a second to realize she meant *dead.*

'Oh.' They were both watching me. I looked away. 'Well . . . I guess I can't meet him, then.'

Beth winced. 'Kathy – I mean, Kat—'

'How did he die?' My fingertips felt like I had dipped them in ice water.

She took a deep breath. 'A heart attack. He lived alone, and the ambulance didn't get there in time . . . You and I had already moved out, you see – I was in the process of getting a divorce from him.'

'Oh,' I said again. I could actually *feel* the black hole inside me, cold and dark and endless. I didn't know what was in it, or how I should feel. Finally I started to eat again. The food tasted like sick in my mouth.

Beth bit her lip. 'Kat, I'm sorry – I should have told you sooner—'

'That's OK.' I could feel her watching me, wanting to say something else. Finally, after a few minutes, she looked down and slowly started eating again too.

No one said anything for a while. We finished the

lasagne, and Beth stood up to clear the plates away. I didn't move as she piled them on top of each other, scraping the leftovers onto the top plate. Then, as she went into the kitchen, I wondered if I used to help her with the dishes.

Used to. Like, just a few days ago. I stared down at my empty place mat, choking back the wet, soggy lump in my throat.

Richard tapped the table. 'You know what?'

I looked at him. 'What?'

He grinned at me. 'Well, since you don't remember anything, you won't have seen my card tricks before – so I can bore you with them all over again.'

I blinked. 'Your what?'

Twisting round in his seat, Richard slid open a drawer in the sideboard and took out a deck of cards. He fanned it across the table. 'Right, I want you to choose a card, but don't show it to me, all right? Just look at it and put it back in the deck.'

The two of clubs. I slid it back into place.

Richard shuffled the deck, splitting the cards into two piles, and then he took a pile and I took one. 'Now, pay attention, because here's where it gets *ve-ery* impressive indeed . . . I want you to look at your bottom card. What is it?'

Slowly, I turned my deck over – and then shook my head, smiling, as I held up the eight of spades. Richard's face fell a million miles.

'Ah,' he said. 'Well, maybe it's at the bottom of *my* pile.' He peeked under his deck like something was about to jump out at him, and then held up the three of hearts with a hopeful expression. 'Is this it?'

'No.' I started to laugh.

'*No?*' Richard twisted his mouth to one side, stroking his sideburns. 'Are you sure? Well, hang on – maybe it's here, behind your ear.'

And he reached across the table and pulled the two of clubs out from my hair.

I stopped laughing as my jaw dropped. 'But – how did you *do* that?' I grabbed the two of clubs from him, turning it over in my hand. It was just a card.

Richard winked at me. Plucking the card from my hand, he shuffled the deck again. 'Magic.'

Later that night I watched TV with Richard and Beth for a while, but it wasn't exactly a success. There was this old movie on called *Casablanca* that Richard said was brilliant, but I couldn't concentrate on it because Beth watched *me* the whole time – with this worried, waiting look on her face.

Occasionally she said things like, 'We watched this together once in Bournemouth, remember?' Or, 'Do you remember what that actor is called, Kat? He's really famous.' She tried to smile and act all casual, but her voice was like a puppy straining at its lead.

I felt like saying, 'Look, I will *let you know* if I remember anything. OK? You'll be the first to know, I promise.'

Instead I just said I was tired, and went upstairs.

Once I got back to my room, I did the exercises for my shoulder that they had taught me in hospital.

They made it hurt worse. Then I went to bed, where I lay awake for ages, reading Kathy's romance novel – it was about a spoiled Spanish princess, and it was incredibly irritating, but better than staring at the walls.

Finally I tossed the book aside and turned out the light, trying not to think about how utterly bizarre this was. I was lying in the same bed that I had slept in for years, but it felt like the first time ever. I wondered if my body remembered it, even if I didn't.

That made me feel seriously squeamish, and my eyes flew open. Which is when I saw it – a green light pulsing on the ceiling, regular as a heartbeat. I snapped the light on again and threw back the covers, peering into the corner where the light was coming from.

A mobile phone attached to a charger lay on the floor, blinking to itself. I flipped it open and sank back on the bed, fiddling with the buttons and trying to remember how to work it. 1 NEW MESSAGE, said the screen.

Date and time . . . no, that wasn't it. Tetris . . . what's Tetris? No, definitely not that either. Eventually I found my way onto a screen that had NEW MESSAGES as an option. Hurrah! I pressed the button.

POPPY'S MOBILE: KATHY R U OK? JADE & I R BOTH SO UPSET, DON'T KNOW WHAT 2 THINK.

Poppy. I had a friend called Poppy, and I must have another one called Jade. Poppy and Jade. My heart quickened. OK, I didn't remember the first thing about either of them, but their names sounded nice. Like they'd be really good laughs.

I pressed the REPLY button, and then stopped, biting my lip. What was I supposed to say? I couldn't very well explain that I had no idea who she was! Or who anyone else was. Including me.

Beth, I decided. I'd show the text to her. If Poppy and Jade were Kathy's friends, then she must know them, right? So maybe I could meet them. The idea bubbled through me. It felt about a million times more exciting than meeting grandparents.

I grabbed a blue dressing gown that was hanging from a hook on the door and went downstairs. I heard voices coming from the kitchen, but I couldn't remember where the light switch was. I edged my way round the black shape of the dining table, feeling more than ever that this wasn't my house and never would be.

I reached for the kitchen door, and then I heard Beth's voice coming from the breakfast nook. 'I know you're right,' she said. 'I just can't help wondering if it's somehow my fault.'

I froze. Leaning forward, I rested my ear against the door.

'I don't think it's anyone's *fault,*' said Richard. 'It's just one of those things that happen, that's all.'

There was a long pause. Finally Beth's voice came again, lower than before. 'Richard, do you know the worst thing? I – I feel like I hardly even know this girl. It's like my daughter's gone.'

'Beth, come on, she's not gone,' said Richard. 'It's probably just temporary; the doctor said so—'

Beth sounded strained. 'But they don't *know,* do

they? They don't even know why she's lost her memory! Oh, Richard, I'm so scared that maybe Kathy won't ever come back, that I'll never see her again – that I've lost my daughter forever—' Her voice broke.

My heart thudding in my ears, I backed away from the door, still holding the mobile. Feeling my way through the shadows, I went back to my room and gently shut the door.

Then I turned out the light and lay there in the dark, curling tightly onto my side and trying not to think of anything at all. I wasn't sure why it hurt so much, hearing Beth say that. I mean, it wasn't like I felt close to her, either.

But I felt so alone, as if I were floating in space. I didn't have anyone, not a single person in the world who really liked me. Well, there was Richard, but he sort of had to, didn't he? There was no one who liked me just for me.

My fingers tightened around the mobile. Except Poppy and Jade, maybe, whoever they were. Please, I thought, clenching my eyes shut. Please let them still be my friends!

Chapter Four

Kathy

16 January
Well, what a great day. I mean, it could not have been any better or more wonderful than this.

The first wonderful thing that happened is that Mum and I had a row. It started because Richard made a big fry-up breakfast for us all – I have no idea why, it's not like it's the weekend or anything. And I can't face that amount of food in the morning anyway, just the smell of it makes me sick. So I told him I wasn't hungry and had some cornflakes instead, and Mum cornered me later and said that I had been really rude.

Which I so totally hadn't been! All I did was tell him I wasn't hungry – what's wrong with that?! But apparently my *tone* was rude and dismissive (Mum's word, can you tell?). She said she knew it must be hard for me having Richard move in, but it's been over two years since she's had a relationship and she deserved a bit of happiness. I thought she was actually going to cry! I mean, my God, all this over a bowl of cornflakes!

I seriously wanted to tell her to CHILL OUT AND LEAVE ME ALONE. But it wasn't worth being banished to my room for the next hundred years, so I just shrugged and said sorry. She made me say sorry to Richard too. I mean, she actually stood there with her arms crossed over her chest until I did it! Richard didn't even *care* that much, I don't think. He just looked sort of embarrassed and said, 'That's OK, Kathy – I should have known how attached you are to your cornflakes.'

By the time I got to school after all that I was practically late, and Tina probably thought I had forgotten about her. She was standing at the front gates looking really anxious. We barely made it to our form room before the bell went.

I did what Mrs Boucher had said, and walked her to all her classes. (They're mostly the same as mine anyway.) We chatted a lot, and were getting on all right. She likes Basingstoke, which was an UTTER shock to me, because Poppy and Jade and I are so bored of the same old shops we could scream. But apparently it's incredibly exciting compared to Shropshire. Remind me never to go to Shropshire!

So it was all going OK . . . until we got to lunch. We sat down with Poppy and Jade and a few of the others, and I introduced Tina to everyone she hadn't met at break. We all just chatted for a while, and then I don't remember how it happened, but someone asked Tina about her parents. 'They're divorced,' she said.

'Oh, that's too bad,' I said. But she said she's really glad about it, actually. Apparently her mum left home a few years ago – just packed her things and left with no warning. So now Tina lives with her dad. But she's totally OK with it, because she has the BEST dad in the whole world (according to her).

She told us all about him. He's an artist who just got a teaching job here, and he also plays the piano. They do jazz duets together, with her on the violin, plus he painted this incredible mural on her bedroom wall for her. She said he's loads of fun and she can talk to him about almost anything.

She went on and on, and with every word she said, I just felt worse. But I couldn't change the subject, because Jade and Poppy were really interested – they kept asking her all these questions about what the mural was like, and what kind of artist her dad was. I could tell they thought he sounded just so cool. Well, he did. He sounded completely wonderful. A total dream-dad.

And to make things even worse *again*, Tina started talking about playing the violin, and how great it is and how much she loves it. I pretended nothing was wrong and just kept smiling with everyone else, but I wasn't saying anything at all by then. I couldn't, I just couldn't.

Then Tina said something like, 'My dad came to my last violin recital, and it was so funny—' and that was it, I couldn't take any more. I said I had to go to the loo, and dashed out before I started crying in front of everyone.

I thought I had got away with it without anyone knowing, but then during PE, Poppy and Jade came over and asked why I had been so rude to Tina!! I asked them what they meant, and it turned out that everyone thought I sounded really snide, the way I said I had to go to the loo and then rushed off.

I couldn't tell them I had been trying not to start bawling in front of the whole canteen, so I shrugged and said, 'Oh, I was just getting tired of hearing her go on about her perfect life.'

Then they both looked at me really strangely. 'I think she's nice,' said Poppy.

'Yeah, how come you don't like nice people any more?' said Jade. 'First Richard, now Tina!'

So I told them I *did* like her, and that I was just in a strange mood. 'You sure are,' said Jade. I wish she would shut up sometimes!!!

17 January

Tina's not acting any different around me, so maybe she didn't think I sounded that snide after all. We were chatting as we walked to class today, and I really do think she's nice, I wasn't just saying that yesterday. Plus she's a good laugh. It's just the way she goes on about things that gets irritating.

I mean, come on. Her dad can't be *that* great. And she's only done her grade three, big deal. I did my grade five when I was ten.

19 January

Why can't Richard just leave me alone?! Why does he have to try to be *friendly* all the time? He practically follows me around, trying to talk to me! When he got home from work today, sure enough, he started right in again – this time showing me one of his card tricks.

Mum was there, so I couldn't just tell him to naff off. I tried to say that I had to go and do my homework, but Mum said, 'Come on, Kathy, just one trick.' With *dire warning* in her voice.

He went through this whole 'Pick a card, any card . . .' routine. I chose the four of diamonds. Then it went back into the deck and he fanned the cards out and put them into different piles and stuff, and then he cut the deck, and it was the four of diamonds.

Well, it's not *that* big a deal. I bet he has the deck marked or something. But he said, 'There, is that your card?' with this big, triumphant grin on his face.

I said, 'No, I chose the jack of spades.' Ha!

He quit smiling and said, 'Really? Are you sure?'

Then Mum tried to laugh. 'Oh, Kathy, quit teasing,' she said. 'Richard always chooses the right card!'

'Well, not this time,' I told them, and went up to my room.

Chapter Five

Kat

'What are your thoughts on fry-ups?' asked Richard. As I came into the kitchen he looked over his shoulder at me with a grin, swirling a saucepan about in his hand. The smells of melting butter and sizzling bacon hung in the air.

'Great,' I said, sliding into a chair. 'It smells really good.'

'It does, doesn't it?' Richard cracked an egg against the side of the pan. 'Help yourself to some orange juice, by the way – you might as well get *something* healthy down you.'

I found the orange juice in the fridge. 'Where's – um, where's my mother?' I said as I poured myself a glass.

Richard glanced at me and I flushed, wishing I hadn't made it so totally obvious that I couldn't call her *Mum.* But I just couldn't; the word wouldn't come. Especially not after what I had overheard last night.

Richard turned back to the hob, prodding at the eggs with a spatula. 'She's taking a shower; she'll be down in a bit. Fancy some toast? Bread's over there; just pop it in the toaster.'

I put the bread in the toaster and then sat down with my juice. Steam from the fry-up coated the windows, making the garden look full of mist. I rubbed a circle on one of the panes and peered out. A patio with some dead pot plants on it, and an overgrown lawn bordered by trees.

'Not at its best this time of year,' said Richard. He clattered forks and knives onto the table, and then loaded up a pair of plates with bacon, eggs, mushroom and tomato. 'Here you go.' He slid a plate in front of me. 'Tuck in while it's hot.'

I picked up the fork, pushing back the sleeves of the black jumper I'd put on that morning. 'Did Kathy only ever use to wear dark colours?' I asked.

Richard stopped eating and looked at me. His eyes were very blue, even in the pale winter light from outside.

'What?' I asked, feeling self-conscious.

He popped a piece of bacon in his mouth. 'Don't you think of yourself as Kathy, then?'

Oh. I shrugged, looking down. 'Not really, I guess. I mean, I know I *am* Kathy, but – I don't know, it just doesn't seem like we have a lot in common so far.'

'Like?' Richard grinned suddenly, pointing at my jumper with his fork. 'Apart from your taste in clothes, that is. And to answer your question, yes, you used to wear a lot of black. You were very into monochromes.'

'What's that?'

'Blacks, whites, greys.'

'And browns,' I pointed out glumly. 'My wardrobe's full of brown too.'

He laughed. 'Well, I don't know if brown is *technically* a monochrome, but yep, that too . . . Go on, I'm curious. How else do you feel different from Kathy?'

Munching on a piece of toast, I told him about the music I had heard in hospital. 'It was so beautiful . . . I even made this girl in the ward change channels back to it, but everyone else hated it. Then, when I saw the CDs in my room, I hoped there might be something like that, but there's only pop.' I lifted a shoulder. 'So we can't be *twins*, exactly, can we?'

Richard smiled. 'I see what you mean.'

I took another bite of toast. 'I wish I knew who wrote that music, though, so I could get the CD.'

'Well, that's easily done. What day was it, Thursday?' Richard hopped up and went into the lounge. A few seconds later he was back, holding a newspaper. He flipped through the pages until he got to the TV section, running his finger down the entries. 'Mahler's Fifth,' he said.

'What?' I craned my neck to see.

'The composer was Gustav Mahler and it's his fifth symphony, known as Mahler's Fifth.' Richard folded the newspaper and handed it to me with a flourish. 'You've got good taste,' he said. 'That's one of my favourites too.'

I held the newspaper, a warm glow filling me. 'Thanks,' I said.

* * *

I helped Richard do the washing-up after we'd eaten, and he told me about a composer called Beethoven. I thought maybe I had heard of him, but I couldn't remember anything he had written, so Richard hummed one of his symphonies for me, conducting an imaginary orchestra with a soapy fork and knife. That was when Beth came into the room.

'Morning,' she said with a smile. It was me she was looking at, though.

'Hi,' I said. My spirits deflated like soapsuds when a greasy pan hits the water. All I could think was, You don't even like me; you just want the old Kathy back.

Beth leaned against the doorway. 'Had a good breakfast?'

I nodded without looking at her. 'Yeah, it was great.'

'Shall I make one for you too?' said Richard, reaching across me to put the spatula on the drying rack. 'It's no bother.'

Beth looked at her watch. 'No, that's OK; I've got a phone appointment in twenty minutes.'

'Right, I'm going to make a move, then,' said Richard. 'I'm going into town for a bit.' He kissed Beth's cheek and winked at me, slapping the door-frame as he left the kitchen.

Beth licked her lips. 'Kat, did you sleep well?'

'Great,' I said. Again.

She poured herself a cup of coffee, glancing at me. 'Did you—?' She stopped.

'What?' I knew what she was going to ask, though. My sore shoulder throbbed as my muscles tightened up.

Beth hesitated, holding the coffee and trying to smile. 'I was just wondering – I mean, you've been home for a day now, and I just wondered if . . . if you've remembered anything. Anything at all,' she added quickly. 'Even if it's really tiny, it might mean something.'

'No,' I said flatly.

'Oh.' Beth forced a laugh. 'Oh, well, it's early days yet . . . I'm sure it'll all be fine.'

I seriously could not bear another second of this conversation. Reaching into my jeans pocket, I pulled out the mobile and flipped it open, pressing the keys until I found the messages section again. I thrust the phone at her. 'Look – I got a text from one of my old friends.'

Beth held the mobile at arm's length, squinting at it. Her face brightened. 'Oh, Poppy! She sounds worried about you, the poor love. What did you say back?'

I leaned against the counter, crossing my arms over my chest. 'Well . . . nothing. I don't remember her. Who is she?'

Beth handed the mobile back to me. 'She's one of your best friends. So's Jade, for that matter. The three of you are practically inseparable. Plus I think there's another girl now, Tina, who you all spend time with.'

It sounded like I had been really popular! I hadn't expected that, for some reason. 'Well . . . do you think I could meet them?'

Beth looked thoughtful for a moment, tapping her lip. 'You know, that's a really good idea . . . They probably know you even better than I do. Talking to them might help you get your memory back.'

I glared at the clean dishes on the drying rack. Why couldn't she just *shut up* about me getting my memory back? OK, yes, it would be a good thing, and I wanted to have it back too – but was I really so awful the way I was now?

Beth rinsed her coffee cup out in the sink and gave it a wipe with the dishcloth. 'I'll give Poppy's mum a ring today. And, Kat . . . what about seeing Nana and Jim meanwhile?'

'Who?' I said. Even though I remembered.

Her mouth tightened worriedly. 'Nana and Jim, my parents. They really want to see you, sweetie. Just to – to make sure you're OK. They're very worried.'

'I'm fine.' I meant that my shoulder and forehead were fine, but Beth gave a short laugh that was almost a bark.

'Well, I wouldn't say you're *fine*, exactly . . . would you?'

My chest tightened, and I looked away. Sorry, I forgot – the only thing that matters is whether I've got my memory back, right?

Beth waited for me to say something, and when I didn't, she sighed. 'Kat, look, we could drive up to see them sometime in the next few days – they're only in Oxfordshire, it's not far. All right?'

'All right,' I muttered.

She squeezed my arm. 'Good. And, Kat—' She broke off, biting her lip.

'What?'

'It'll all be fine,' she said softly. 'I promise.'

I took a shower that afternoon. I wasn't actually *supposed* to take a shower, because of the bandage that was still on my forehead, but I was desperate to wash my hair – it felt like an oil slick had been spilled over it. I tipped my head back carefully as I rubbed the shampoo in, savouring the coconut smell.

Afterwards, I towel-dried my hair, staring at myself in the mirror. It was still a shock every time I caught sight of myself, like seeing a stranger looking back at me. A stranger who was starting to look sort of familiar, maybe, but still a stranger.

'It'll all be fine,' I whispered to my reflection. Echoes of Beth.

The girl in the mirror didn't say anything.

'Well, Kathy, how are you finding things at home?' Dr Perrin smiled her toothy smile at me, like she was about to snap me up in her jaws.

'Kat,' I told her, chewing on a nail.

She glanced down at her notes. 'Oh, Kat – sorry. Right, how are you finding things at home, Kat?' She smiled at me again, showing even more teeth. If that were possible.

I shifted on the sagging green sofa. I was in Dr Perrin's office at the hospital because, just my luck, she was going to see me once a week until my memory came back. Or until we had reached 'a good status quo', whatever that meant.

'Things are OK,' I told her.

Dr Perrin scribbled something on her clipboard. Her honey-coloured hair was just as bright as before, framing her face in a hair-sprayed wave. 'Can you expand on that?'

'Um . . . well, they're OK. I mean, everything's going fine.' Her desk and walls were filled with photos of toothily smiling people. I stared at a photo of a little girl in a fairy dress. Her smile would scare off a shark.

She tapped her pen against her teeth. 'I see. Any memories coming back to you yet?'

'No, not really.'

Dr Perrin leaned forward. 'Not really? Does that mean you *have* remembered something?'

I swallowed, tugging at my sleeves. 'No, um . . . it means no.'

Dr Perrin let out a breath, and then gave me a big smile. 'Let's try to be precise, Kat. Now, then – what about your dreams? Do you remember any of them?'

I shrugged, thinking of a dream I'd had just the night before. I had looked in the mirror, and instead of my stranger-face looking back at me, there hadn't been any face at all – just a smooth, flesh-coloured blank. Goosebumps prickled across my arms as I remembered it.

I was not about to share this with Dr Perrin.

'Is that a yes or a no?' she was saying. 'Kat, dear, we must try to be exact. We are investigators, working together to unlock your memory, and we can leave *no stone unturned.*'

I stared at her in disbelief. An image of the two of

us creeping along with magnifying glasses flashed into my mind, and I cringed.

'Do you understand?' asked Dr Perrin.

'Um, I think so,' I muttered. Thinking, I understand that you are a total loon.

She crossed her plump legs, leaning forward. 'Good. Because you see, your dreams could be very, very important in overcoming your memory loss; this has been proven time and again in cases like this. So it's essential that we—'

'No,' I told her.

Her eyebrows shot up. 'I beg your pardon?'

'I mean . . . the answer's no. I don't remember any dreams.'

She sighed, and wrote down something else. Another big, scary smile. 'Fine. Now then, I'm going to show you a series of images, and I want you to tell me the first things that come to mind. OK? We're just going to free-associate. It'll be fun.'

It sounded like she was giving me an order: *Have fun or else.* I pressed back against the sofa, longing for the time to be up.

It was like that for the whole forty-five minutes. And I know it was forty-five minutes precisely, because I was watching the clock like a hawk. Finally Dr Perrin said, 'Well, I think that's all for now, Kat,' and I leaped up from the sofa.

She pinned me in place with her eyes. 'You'll remember to keep a dream diary,' she said sternly. 'Every morning, without fail. We'll go over them at our next session.'

I gulped and nodded. Standing up, I could see that her eyebrows were drawn on with a pencil. I gazed at them, weirdly fascinated. Where had her actual eyebrows gone?

'You won't forget,' Dr Perrin said as she opened the door and showed me out. It wasn't a question.

Chapter Six

Kathy

23 January
I wonder how long this FAB buddy thing is meant to last for. Tina doesn't need me to show her to her classes any more, she knows where they all are. *And* she knows all my friends now. In fact, she's getting on so well with Poppy and Jade that I feel like a total outsider. They've started walking to class with her too. Usually there's not enough space for all four of us to walk side by side, so guess who ends up walking behind.

Well, I might as well, I don't feel like talking to anyone anyway.

25 January
I got a C on my English paper. I usually get As in English. At least it wasn't maths, which Richard's already offered to help me with – NO, THANK YOU!

26 January
I asked Mrs Boucher how long the FAB thing lasted, and she said it would be nice if I kept doing it until the end of term. Nice for who??

I said, 'But Tina knows her way to all her classes now,' and she said, 'Oh, you don't need to keep walking to class with her. Just be there as a support if she needs you.'

So that's one good thing, at least. Not that Tina will even notice if I walk to class with her or not.

27 January

Jade asked me how long I planned to keep sulking about Richard moving in. Then she said, 'Or is it Tina's perfect life you're sulking about now?' Poppy didn't say, 'Oh, Jade,' this time.

I said I wasn't sulking, I'd just got a lot on my mind. I could tell neither of them believed me.

At home things are pretty much the same as they were too. Mum keeps saying that I'm not making enough of an effort. It's not like I'm sticking pins in a Richard voodoo doll or anything! The real problem is that she wants me to play Happy Families with her and Richard, and it's just *so* not going to happen. I don't like Richard and I don't like him being here, so why should I pretend I do?

But to *make an effort*, I told him thank you for making dinner tonight. Big mistake. He thought I was his friend at last, and wanted me to go into the lounge with him so he could teach me one of his stupid card tricks. I said no thanks, and then got in trouble off Mum again for being 'unfriendly'. I can't win.

I took Cat out tonight, and sat holding him for a long time. He didn't make me feel any better, though. I just kept thinking about Dad.

28 January
It's Saturday today. Normally I would have made plans with Poppy and Jade, but no one mentioned anything about getting together this weekend, so I didn't, either. I'm not actually that bothered about it, because I don't really want to see them anyway. I'm too busy *sulking*, ha ha.

I wonder if they're doing anything with Tina?

Later
Mum came into my room, and made me turn down my music. She said she wanted to talk to me, so right away I knew it wasn't going to be anything good. It wasn't, either. She sat on my bed and said that she really did understand how I must feel (I wish she'd stop saying that!) but that life has to go on. And that *her* life has moved on, and now it includes Richard, and she'd very much like for my life to include Richard too.

'Can't you just try?' she said.

I told her that I *was* trying, but that I didn't see why I had to include Richard in my life just because he was her boyfriend. I said it very calmly, but her face turned red anyway.

'Because he lives here!' she said.

'Well, that's not *my* fault,' I said back.

Big mistake, the row was on. She said she had tried to be patient, but I was being incredibly self-involved, and it was time I grew up a little and tried thinking of someone else for a change. On and on and on, with her face getting redder and redder, and I could hardly even listen to her because it was SO TOTALLY UNFAIR. God! She *knew* I didn't want him to move in, but she went ahead and asked him to anyway – and now she's all upset that I'm not happy about it! Well, whose fault is that?!

Finally I just lost it, and started shouting at her. I told her I never wanted him to move in, and I've had enough of him trying to talk to me and get on my good side, he is NOT my dad, and I don't want anything to do with him! I almost started crying, but I didn't, I managed to hold it in.

Mum looked like she was going to start yelling back at me, but then her shoulders slumped and she just sighed. She said, 'Kathy, I can't change what happened with your dad. I'm sorry that things worked out the way they did.'

'Worked out.' That's a funny way of putting it, since our leaving was all down to her. I know that things weren't always that great, but surely we could have coped?? If she had really wanted to?? And then everything might have been different.

Anyway, she asked me to please try harder with Richard, and I said I would (just to get rid of her), and FINALLY she went away and left me alone. I turned my music back up again the second she did. I just want to block out the whole world.

Chapter Seven

Kat

Nana and Jim lived in a village called Upper Bagley. It was only about two hours away, but it felt like centuries. I spent the whole drive staring out of the window, wishing that Richard hadn't had to go to work that day. Beth kept tapping her fingers on the steering wheel and fiddling with the car radio, changing the station every five minutes or so.

Nana turned out to be an older version of Beth – and me, I suppose. Weird thought. When we got there, she gave me a quick hug and then held me away from her at arm's length, gripping my shoulders and looking into my eyes. I stiffened, waiting for the inevitable *do you remember?* questions.

She dropped her hands and smiled at me. 'Would you like something to drink?'

I was so relieved that I said yes, even though I wasn't thirsty. Nana disappeared into the kitchen, and I was just thinking, Maybe this won't be so bad after all, when Beth steered me into the lounge.

A woman and two men sat watching TV. The moment we walked in, everyone's eyes snapped towards me and they all jumped up, beaming big smiles.

'Kathy!'

'Are you all right, love?'

'How are you, Kath?'

Suddenly I was being passed about from one to the other, given bone-crunching hugs. The old man squeezed me the tightest, thumping my back like I was choking on something. I tried not to yelp as pain shot through my shoulder.

'Now, what's all this nonsense about you not remembering anything?' he boomed. 'Eh? Are you saying you don't remember your Grandad Jim?'

'Um . . .' Completely panicked, I looked across at Beth.

'I'm afraid not, Dad.' She pulled off her coat and put it on the beige-coloured settee.

Grandad Jim stared at me. 'You really don't remember anything?'

'I'm sorry,' I whispered. Fire crept up my neck and cheeks.

'You don't *remember* me?!' His eyes goggled as his voice rose. If he had been holding a cane, he would have thumped it on the floor.

'She obviously doesn't, Dad,' said the other man. He had thinning brown hair, and a crooked smile. 'Sorry if we sort of attacked you before,' he said to me. 'I'm your Uncle Mark. Your mum's older brother.'

'And I'm your Aunt Lorraine,' offered the woman. 'Rainey.' Blonde hair and a bright blue jumper. She gave me her hand, and I shook it, trying to smile.

'Oh, your poor head!' she said, peering at my forehead. 'Does it hurt?'

The bandage was off by then, but the stitches were still there, stark and black against my skin. I had tried to brush my hair over them that morning, which obviously hadn't worked.

'Um, not too bad —' I started to say.

'This is ridiculous!' bawled Grandad Jim in the centre of the room. 'The girl can't have just *lost her memory!*'

Beth shrugged, looking tired. 'Nevertheless . . . she has.'

Grandad Jim sank into a chair, glaring at her. 'Well, has she seen a doctor? What's being done for her, what's happening?'

Beth sat on the sofa. 'She's seeing a psychiatrist. But Dad, it's not—'

'A *shrink*?' Grandad Jim looked horrified. 'But it could be a brain tumour! Has anyone *checked*?'

Hugging myself, I perched on a round cushion in the corner, wishing it were a magic teleport system that would whisk me away. Beth looked like she was wishing pretty much the same thing about the sofa.

'No, Dad, she definitely doesn't have brain damage. It's a psychological condition. This is what the doctors recommend.'

A psychological condition. There was a beat as everyone looked at me. I shifted on the cushion, trying to look as un-psychotic as possible. Thankfully, Nana came into the room just then, carrying a black enamel tray. A shiny silver tea set was spread out on it.

'Ooh, the posh stuff,' said Mark, jumping up to help her.

Waving him off, Nana set the tray onto the coffee table and handed me a glass of juice. 'Here you go, love. Just how you like it.'

I struggled to smile at her. 'Thanks.' Then I took a sip of the juice, and suddenly my smile was real. 'This is really nice!'

She nodded briskly, pouring herself a cup of tea. 'Freshly squeezed. Nothing at all like that concentrated mess you get at the supermarket.'

'What about the accident, then?' barked Grandad Jim suddenly. 'What happened with that?' I froze, the orange juice chilling my hand.

Beth cleared her throat. 'Apparently Kathy ran in front of the car . . . We think she was probably trying to cross against the lights.'

He looked aghast. 'Cross against the *lights*? Surely she knows better than that!'

'Maybe she was just in a hurry,' said Rainey brightly.

For a few minutes, the only sound was the clinking of cups and saucers. Beth looked over at me and gave me a little smile. I didn't smile back. How could she have brought me here? She must have known what it would be like!

It got worse. After everyone had finished their tea, Grandad Jim hauled out about a hundred photo albums and even a couple of home videos, and everyone crowded around me, pointing out this person and that person, and my first Christmas, and on and on.

'Look, Kathy, do you remember this?' Uncle Mark pointed to a photo of me on a tricycle. 'We went outside and I pushed you on it, all up and down the pavement. Remember?'

'No.' I thought the girl in the photo looked a bit fed up too. Maybe she had wanted to tell Uncle Mark to stop pushing her and leave her alone.

'*Here's* one you'll know,' said Rainey, dimpling like she had the prize answer to a contest. 'Look – who's this?' She held up a photo of a man standing on the beach, wearing shorts and a blue T-shirt. His arms were folded across his chest.

'I don't know.' My voice sounded completely flat.

The smile dropped from her face. 'Kathy, it's your dad!'

'Oh.' I slowly took the photo from her. My dad. He was a stocky brown-haired man with intense eyes. The word *proud* popped into my head. And he looked strong, like if you started to drown in the ocean he'd dive in and rescue you.

Rainey gave a forced laugh, trying to make a joke out of it. 'Oh dear, you don't even know your dad! Never mind, we—'

My hand trembled, and I threw the photo down onto the pile. 'No! I don't! I don't know *any* of you, OK?'

Beth looked pained. 'Kat—'

I jumped up, scattering albums and photos. 'No! Just leave me alone, why can't you!'

Nana stood up in a single motion, smoothing her palms over her trousers. 'Kathy, would you like to come for a walk with me? I rather fancy some fresh air.'

There was a canal not far from their house, it turned out. Nana and I walked along the towpath in silence, our feet squelching in the soft mud. The water lapped against the edges of the path as I breathed in the crisp March air, looking at the winter skeletons of the trees.

'It must be so pretty here in the springtime,' I said.

Nana nodded, tilting her head back as she looked at the trees. 'Yes. I rather like it all year round, actually.' A log had fallen across the path, and Nana climbed over it, holding one of the branches down for me as I followed her.

She glanced at me. 'You know, people will always want to focus on the whys and wherefores – but the most important thing isn't so much what happened then, but what you do now.'

I frowned. 'What do you mean?'

A strand of greying hair fell across her forehead. 'Well, it seems to me that you've been given a great gift, in a way.'

My jaw dropped. A gift? She was barking! 'But I don't know anything about who I am! I'm just this – this *void.* Beth is always trying to get me to remember things, and I *can't,* and then she gets upset, and it's all just completely awful!' The words came spilling out, like a waterfall crashing over rocks.

Nana shook her head. 'Oh, Kathy, of course it's difficult! But think about it; you're seeing life in a way few people ever get to – completely unencumbered by all the baggage we normally carry. New, fresh; like you've only just been born.'

I didn't have an answer to that. Finally I turned away, watching a leaf swirl its way down the canal. Nana stood beside me, her shoulder almost touching mine as we watched it dip and turn with the current.

New, I thought. Fresh. I tipped my head back and looked at the sky.

'I wish—' I stopped abruptly. A small brown bird landed in a tangle of bracken on the bank, and stood twittering at us, bobbing its tail up and down.

Nana looked at me. 'What?'

I had been about to say that I wished I could live here with Nana instead of with Beth, but that probably wouldn't go down too well. Beth was Nana's daughter after all. And it was a mad thought anyway. I seriously would *not* want to live in the same house with Grandad Jim.

'I just – I wonder what my dad was like,' I said. I looked quickly at her. I hadn't expected to say that, but now that I had, it was true.

Nana was silent for a long moment, watching the water move lazily past. A small muscle in her jaw moved. 'Your father could be the most charming man on the planet,' she said finally. 'Certainly Beth thought so when she married him. We all did.'

A thread of steel ran through her voice. I opened my mouth to ask what she meant, and then closed it again. I wasn't sure I wanted to know.

Nana seemed to stir from somewhere deep within

herself. She smiled, and touched my shoulder. 'Come on. We should probably get back now; we've been gone a long time.'

'Right, now this is the tricky part,' said Richard. 'Once you've got their card on top of the deck you have to palm it, like this.' He held up his hand, showing me the deck. Then, with a twitch of his little finger, the top card popped up and cupped itself against his palm.

'I'll never be able to do that!' I said. We were sitting on the lounge floor, the TV on in the background. Beth sat on the sofa behind us, flipping through a knitting magazine and trying not to look like she was listening to every word.

'Sure you will,' said Richard. 'It's not as hard as it looks. Here, take the deck and hold it like this.' He arranged my hand around the deck. 'Got it? Right, now press your little finger against the top right corner and pull the card towards you.'

I pulled the card towards me. The deck seemed to explode in my hand, with cards fluttering all around my feet. 'That's not exactly what you meant is it?' I said.

He laughed. 'Well, you won't get it in a day; you have to practise. Come on, again.'

I glanced over at the TV as I swept the cards together. Some sort of school programme was on – a group of girls in green uniforms stood clustered together in a corridor, talking excitedly. *Poppy and Jade,* I thought, and twisted round.

'Beth, I was just wondering – did you ring Poppy's mum?'

Her chin jerked up. She stared at me from over the top of the magazine, her eyes wide and startled. 'What?'

I blinked, confused. 'Um . . . I was just wondering if . . .' I trailed off, realizing that I had called her *Beth*.

She put down the magazine. Her cheeks were red. She started to say something, and then stopped, biting her lip.

'Sorry,' I whispered. 'It just – popped out.'

She shook her head quickly. 'No, no, that's OK . . . I mean, if that's what you want to call me.' She tried to smile. 'Sorry . . . what did you ask me?'

Sprawled out on the floor across from me, Richard sat very still, gazing at Beth with concern. Guilt punched me. *How* could I have been so stupid?

Beth was still looking at me, waiting.

'Um . . . I was just wondering about Poppy and Jade,' I said, fiddling with a card. 'Whether they're coming over or not.'

She nodded. 'Yes, I meant to tell you – they're coming tomorrow afternoon. Poppy's mum is going to bring Jade over as well. Excuse me, I – I just think I'll get a cup of tea.'

She jumped up from the sofa and disappeared into the kitchen. Richard unfolded himself quickly from the floor and went after her, squeezing my shoulder as he went.

I sat there among the brightly coloured cards, staring down at them. The kings and queens and jacks were all scattered, facing in different directions. I gathered the deck together and put it away. I didn't feel like practising any more.

Chapter Eight

Kathy

29 January

I think Mum said something to Richard, because he hasn't been talking to me as much since yesterday. He still smiles at me, but he's stopped making his stupid jokes and trying to show me his card tricks all the time. Thank God.

I went for a swim this afternoon. I sort of thought I might see Poppy at the pool, since she goes on Sundays sometimes, but I didn't. I wasn't really looking out for her anyway – I was concentrating on my swimming. I did thirty-two lengths.

30 January

I'm trying really hard to show a happy face at school now, since it's obvious that I won't have any friends left soon if I don't. It seems to be working, sort of. I sat with Poppy and Jade and Tina at lunch today, and pretended everything was wonderful and I was having a fantastic time. I don't know if I managed to convince *myself* of it, but everyone else looked pleased.

I seriously wish Mrs Boucher had picked someone

else for Tina's FAB buddy, though. She's so stuck on herself! I don't know why Poppy and Jade can't see it. Why do they think she's so great? She just goes *on* about her wonderful perfect father, and the violin. Every other word that comes out of her mouth is, 'I'm so artistic, I'm so wonderful, me me me!'

It's actually really weird, because Jade is usually the last person to put up with that sort of rubbish. I wonder why she can't see it in Tina??

Anyway, I pretended that I like Tina as much as Poppy and Jade do, and the four of us had a really good laugh over lunch, even if Tina did keep blabbing on about her wonderful life. (Yes, thank you, we're all so interested!)

Jade nudged me as we were throwing our rubbish away, and said, 'See? It's not so hard, is it?' I told her I didn't know what she was talking about. But at least we're all getting on again, and if Tina has to be included in that, then I guess I'll just have to deal with it.

31 January

Still keeping up the happy face at school. I'm not bothering much at home, though.

'Home', that's a laugh. It doesn't feel like my home any more. I can't go *anywhere* in the house without Richard being there. Mum and I used to watch TV together at night, and we never do any more, because I can't stomach the sight of her curled up with loverboy on the settee. They don't kiss or anything in front of me, but—

That was SO close! Mum walked in just as I was writing that last line. I had Cat out from his hiding place, and I just barely managed to shove him under my pillow before Mum saw. She definitely saw that I was writing in a journal, though, and I could tell she was ACHING to know what about, even though she pretended to be all laid-back and casual. She said there was a special about penguins on, and did I want to come watch it. I used to really like penguins.

I told her maybe later (trying to sound pleasant), and she looked like she wanted to say something else, but then finally she left. I've put Cat back in his hiding place now. It just would not be worth the aggro if Mum ever saw him. There would be so many questions, and it's nothing to do with her, actually.

I'll have to find a better hiding place for this journal too. I don't trust her not to go snooping around and trying to read it, though *of course* she'd say she just happened to see it by mistake, or only read it because she was so worried about me.

Maybe I will go and watch some of that special. So long as I can sit far away from the lovebirds and don't have to talk to them.

1 February

Tina's asked Poppy, Jade and me to sleep over at her house on Friday night. Poppy and Jade are both so excited they're practically jumping up and down. I acted excited too, but said I wasn't sure if I could, and I'd have to ask Mum. Jade laughed and said, 'Are you mad? OF COURSE she'll say yes, she'd probably kill to get a night alone with Richard!'

Which made me feel even worse.

2 February

Tina's father dropped her off at school today, and we all got to meet him. He looks really young, and he has long blond hair in a ponytail! He was OK, I guess. I mean, he said hello to us and seemed friendly enough, but he was nothing to write home about.

Poppy and Jade were completely smitten, of course. After he drove off they kept gushing on about how nice he is, and how lucky Tina is. And Tina, totally stuck on herself as usual, gave this big grin and said, 'I know.' It was all I could do not to say something really sarcastic to her.

The urge got worse as the day went on, because the big topic of conversation today was the sleepover at Tina's tomorrow night. I'm not joking, *every last detail* has been discussed. What we'll be eating, doing, even thinking! They're planning on getting a pizza and renting some DVDs, plus Tina said that she and her dad have a set of bongos and some castanets and stuff, and we can all have a midnight jam session! With her on the violin, of course.

Poppy and Jade have *never* been into music before – I mean, not into playing it – but they were falling all over themselves about how much FUN that sounded. Hurrah, we'll get to listen to Tina on the violin, showing off.

I felt like telling them that she can't be *that* good, she's only grade three! But they don't even know that I used to play, and there's no way I'm going to mention it to them. They'd ask loads of questions, and I really don't want to explain any of it.

I haven't asked Mum yet about tomorrow night. I don't want to go, to be honest – I get enough of Tina at school. But I didn't want anyone to think I was *sulking* again, so when Poppy asked me if I had told Mum about it yet, I said yes, and that she was thinking it over. Then Jade gave me a funny look and asked what she had to think about.

'I don't know,' I said. 'I guess she's worried because she doesn't know Tina's dad. She can be sort of funny about that kind of thing.'

Which was a mistake, because then Tina said, 'Oh, that's no problem, my dad can ring her.' So I had to back-pedal like mad, and say she'd probably say yes after all, and the best thing to do was just leave her alone and she'd come around.

Jade kept saying, 'No, ring her now, let's get it sorted so you can come!' WHY does she always have to stick her nose in?! Finally I told them that Mum wasn't home today, and that her mobile's broken. I'm not sure if Jade believed me. I saw her raising her eyebrows at Poppy.

She made me promise to ask Mum again the second I saw her tonight. Which I haven't done – I've been home for hours now, and I haven't mentioned it to her.

I don't think I'm going to go, actually. I've got sort

of a stomach-ache, I think I'm coming down with something. In fact, I think I should probably just stay in bed tomorrow.

3 February

I got a text from Jade at 10.20 a.m. on the dot (morning break!), asking why I wasn't in school. I texted back that I had a virus, and Mum was making me stay at home. And that I was really, really upset that I couldn't make the party tonight.

She wrote back: YR FAKING IT, AREN'T U?

And I said: NO, HONEST! FEEL AWFUL. SAY SOZ 2 TINA FOR ME.

Then she wrote: OK, C U MONDAY THEN, so I think she believed me. Hopefully. Besides, I really am ill! My stomach's been hurting like mad all last night and today. Even Mum believed me, and I can't fake anything past her.

Anyway, what a fab day. A good rest, just what I needed. I'm lying snuggled up on the settee in my dressing gown now, covered up with the spare duvet and watching TV (Richard's at work, hurrah!). Mum's been popping downstairs every hour or so between her phone appointments to see how I am. It feels nice, like it's just the two of us again. She's just made me some of her herbal tea to settle my stomach. Most of them are foul, but some of the berry ones are OK.

Later

Richard brought me a bunch of flowers home from work! He gave them to me with a big flourish and said,

'Hope you feel better soon.' I could feel my cheeks go all red, how stupid is that?! I wanted to say, 'Nice try at buying my affections, better luck next time.' Instead I just mumbled, 'Thank you.' Mum made a big fuss over how pretty they are, and put them in a vase for me. They're by my bed now – roses and daises and some other flowers. They *are* sort of pretty, I guess. But he's still a jerk.

It's after 10.00 at night now, so I guess everyone's having a fantastic time at Tina's. I'm SO glad that I'm ill and couldn't go.

I'd sort of like to hear Tina play the violin, though. Just to see if she's any good.

4 February

I've gone back to bed. I thought I was fine this morning, so Mum let me go into town, but I seriously wish I had stayed home, even with Richard there all day. When she picked me up this afternoon I told her that I probably hadn't been well enough after all, and she felt my forehead and said that I was a bit flushed.

So now I'm curled up in bed, trying not to cry. I won't, though. Mum could walk in with some tea or something for me any second.

What's *wrong* with me?! It's not like anything bad happened! I was just wandering around, looking at the shops. It felt so weird being in town on a Saturday by myself. Usually I've got Poppy and Jade with me, and we end up in Ben and Jerry's, seeing who can get the weirdest combination of flavours. I didn't go in there today, because obviously I wasn't about to sit stuffing my face with ice cream on my own.

Somehow I ended up in the old part of town. We don't usually go there because the shops are awful, but since I was there I bought a sausage roll at the bakery. And then I just happened to be passing by the music shop, and since I didn't have anything better to do I went inside.

There were a bunch of boys in there drooling over the guitars, but no one I knew. The violins were on display in the back, on these special stands. Some of them were just so beautiful – gleaming this rich, warm brown colour. Then the man in the shop asked me if I played, and I said no and got out in a hurry.

I don't know why I went in there. It was stupid, it's nothing to do with me any more. And now, for some mad reason, I can't stop thinking of this recital I gave when I was ten. The Brahms piece keeps going through my head, over and over. It was really lovely. I used to know it inside out. I still do, in my head.

Why did Dad say that? *Why?* I had worked so hard, and I thought I did really well. Mrs Patton, my teacher, thought so too. She gave me this massive hug when I got off stage, and said, 'Well done!'

But then no one said anything in the car on the way home, there was just this awful silence. Until finally Dad said it: 'You know, I've never liked classical music much. God, it's boring.'

Mum's cheeks got really red, but she stood up for me, going on about how well I had done, and how could he *say* that. I just sat in the back, hardly even moving – it was like I had turned to stone. I didn't know if he was going to smack her, or what. I was gripping my violin case, and I remember feeling so exposed and *naked* holding it – like, here I am with my little violin, how utterly sad. A small part of me actually felt sorry for my violin too, like Dad had hurt its feelings or something.

Daft daft daft.

Anyway, I keep thinking about that. I don't know why. OK, Dad was being a jerk, but I've got *loads* of memories of him being a jerk, so why this particular one is bothering me so much, I don't know.

I *am* crying now. Bugger.

Chapter Nine

Kat

Discarded tops lay around my room – one on the bed, one hanging off the back of the chair, one draped over the computer where I had thrown it.

I pawed through my wardrobe, the coat hangers clicking together. I didn't really know why I was still looking. I already knew exactly what was in there, and unless helpful little clothes fairies had visited during the night, it wouldn't have changed.

They hadn't. There are never clothes fairies around when you need them.

Finally I pulled out a brown v-neck top, and sighed. Putting it on, I gazed at myself in the mirror. Maybe a red hair band, to brighten things up a bit? Not that Kathy would have one, of course. Far too cheerful.

It doesn't matter! I yelled at myself. Poppy and Jade must have seen you wearing these clothes zillions of times; they're not going to care!

I cared, though. I wanted them to see me as Kat, not Kathy.

Glancing at the clock, I pulled open one of the

desk drawers. A hotch-potch of pens, old CDs, half-used nail varnish. So Kathy was secretly untidy! I rummaged quickly through it, and was just about to give up when my fingers closed on a green hair band. Victory!

I twisted my hair back, fastening it. The splash of green didn't liven things up all that much, to be honest, but it was better than nothing. I banged the drawer shut, wishing I had time to paint my nails.

A clattering noise as something fell. Sliding the drawer open again, I peered behind it. There was a sort of space back there, like a dark cavity that went down to the carpet. It looked like a CD had fallen into it.

Beth's voice floated up the stairs. 'Kat! Poppy and Jade are here!'

My heart crashed against my ribs. I shoved the drawer back into place and glanced at myself in the mirror. I *wished* the stitches weren't still in my forehead; I looked like a zombie or something. I pulled quickly at my fringe, trying to cover them up. At least the cut wasn't so red and awful-looking around the edges any more.

Relax! I told myself. *Come on, it'll be fine. These are your friends!*

I put on a smile and went downstairs.

Two girls were sitting in the lounge, side by side on the sofa. One of them had long black hair, and the other a mop of blonde curls. They looked even more nervous than I felt. We all just sort of looked at each other, until finally Beth took over.

'Kat, this is Jade—' She put a hand on the dark-haired girl's shoulder. 'And this is Poppy.' She nodded to the blonde.

'Hi,' I said.

Poppy licked her lips, glancing at my forehead. 'Hi.' A nervous giggle bubbled out of her.

Jade looked down at her feet. A long lock of shiny black hair fell over her shoulders.

'Right, I'll just go and get you some drinks,' said Beth. 'Won't be a moment.' She disappeared into the kitchen.

I kept staring at Jade, suddenly realizing that she looked familiar. She actually looked familiar! I had seen her before; I was sure of it. Where, though? Was it a memory from when I was Kathy?

Poppy licked her lips. Her blue eyes were stretched wide, almost scared. 'Kathy – I mean, Kat – you really don't remember being friends with us?'

I shook my head. 'No, I don't think so.' Sitting down beside them on the sofa, I glanced across at Jade. 'It's weird, though – I sort of feel like I've seen you before, but I don't know where.'

Jade's mouth twisted a bit. 'Really?'

'I think so.'

'You remember me, huh?' She looked at Poppy.

I frowned, not sure what her tone meant. 'Um . . . I'm not sure. I think maybe I do.'

'But nothing else?'

I shook my head slowly, wondering what she was getting at.

'Right, here we go,' said Beth, coming back in

from the kitchen. 'Cokes and biscuits all round.' She put a tray onto the coffee table, her dark fringe falling across her forehead as she leaned down.

'Thanks, Miss Yates,' said Poppy, reaching for a biscuit. Jade took a Coke.

Beth hovered on the sidelines for a few moments, smiling brightly. When nobody said anything, she let out a breath and said, 'Well – I suppose I'll go do some work, and let you girls chat in private.'

The three of us sat like birds on a wire as she went upstairs, not moving until the sound of her study door closing floated down. Then Jade looked at me, flipping her hair back. 'So you don't remember anything else at all?'

I shook my head. 'No.'

Her eyes cut towards Poppy again. 'Really? Not about *anything*?'

Irritation flicked at me. Suddenly I knew where I had seen Jade before. 'I remember you,' I said. 'You were there after I was hit by the car. There was this ginger-haired girl who was crying, and you had your arm around her, saying something to her.'

Jade slowly sat up. Her eyes hardened. 'Yeah, I was there. Why are you leaving Poppy out, though? *She* was there too.'

Poppy? I looked at her, trying to remember. 'You were?'

Her cheeks blazed. She stared down at the sofa, playing with a loose thread. 'Um . . . yeah. I told the ambulance people your name.'

It came back in a rush. Along with the sideways

glances they had all given each other before anyone had said anything.

'Right,' I said. 'I remember.'

Poppy looked away, rubbing her hands in her lap. The three of us sat shifting on the sofa for what felt like centuries. Jade had her legs crossed, and kept tapping her foot like there was music playing. I couldn't tell what either of them were thinking, and it was making me more and more nervous.

Finally Poppy cleared her throat. 'Um, Kat . . . is it really weird, not remembering anything?' Her voice sounded thin.

Jade snorted. 'Yeah, *weird* is the word,' she muttered.

The muscles in my shoulder gave a painful twinge. 'What do you mean?'

She drummed her fingers on the sofa. 'Because amnesia sounds like some stupid movie on TV, that's why. And it's just a little too *convenient* for you to have it, don't you think? Especially now.'

Poppy licked her lips. 'Jade, maybe—'

'Oh, come on! You don't *believe* this!' Jade glanced at the stairs, and lowered her voice. 'After what happened, you can't think she's actually telling the truth!'

'I am!' I burst out. 'I have amnesia; you can ask my doctors!'

Jade gave an unpleasant laugh. 'Yeah, like we're really going to do that. Anyway, it can't be too hard to fake! You just keep saying, *I don't remember, I don't remember!*' She wagged her head, making her voice high-pitched and sing-songy. A chill shuddered up my spine.

'Shut *up*, Jade!' Poppy leaned forward. 'What about Tina? Do you remember anything about her?'

I swallowed. 'I think my mother mentioned her . . . Is she a friend of mine?' Unlike you two, I added in my head.

Jade blew out a breath. 'A friend of yours – um, yeah, I don't *think* so.' She whirled towards Poppy. 'Please tell me you're not falling for this innocent act! Not after what I told you!'

Poppy sat back against the sofa, staring at me. 'I don't know,' she said. 'It does seem pretty—'

'Pretty *what*?' I jumped up. I couldn't bear sitting so close to either of them for a moment longer. 'What are you both on about?'

'I think you know, actually.' Jade's face reddened. 'I think you know exactly! Maybe you fooled your doctors and your mum and everyone else, but you don't fool us, *Miss Amnesia*. God, you make me sick!'

She stood up, grabbing a small black bag. 'You want to know what I was saying to that *ginger-haired girl*, by the way? I was telling her that it was *not* our fault that you ran out into the road.'

I stared at her. '*Your* fault? But – why would it be?'

'Because you saw us and ran for it, that's why,' snapped Jade.

My hands turned to ice. 'Why would I do that?'

'Hmm, well, let me see. *Maybe* you were afraid of what we might do to you. And maybe you were totally right. Come on, Poppy. I've seriously had enough of this.'

Poppy nodded, looking grim. 'Yeah, I guess we better go now.'

Jade yanked on her coat, flipping her hair out from under the collar and crossing the strap of her bag over her chest. 'Come on, Pop . . . we can walk into town from here, and your mum can pick us up.'

I followed them to the front door, feeling dazed, like a tornado had just blown through the house. 'But I don't understand – I mean, I thought you were supposed to be my friends . . .'

Jade ignored me, wrapping her scarf around her neck. My fingernails bit into my palms. 'Look, why did you even come, if you hate me so much?'

She shot me a slitty-eyed glance. 'Because my mother made me,' she said coldly. 'And I wasn't about to tell her what happened. *Some* people keep their promises.'

'Bye,' muttered Poppy as they left.

I grabbed her arm. 'Poppy, wait! What's going on? Won't you tell me?'

She yanked sharply away from me. 'I think Jade's right – you already know. And it's really disgusting of you, Kathy.' She hurried to catch up with Jade, buttoning her coat as she went.

Beth didn't hear them go – that was the only good thing. I poured the rest of the Cokes down the sink and put the biscuits back in the pack. Then I sat perched on the edge of the sofa, biting a nail and trying to work out what had happened.

They hated me, that was totally obvious. But why? They were meant to be my friends! I rubbed my arms, feeling cold. Had I really been so scared of them that I had run out into traffic?

I swallowed hard. Maybe I hadn't even *had* any friends.

My head snapped up as I heard Beth coming downstairs. Rushing to the sideboard, I grabbed Richard's deck of cards and quickly spread them out on the dining table. When she entered the room, I was dealing them out to myself, practising the card trick.

She looked around, her face almost comically surprised. 'Where are Poppy and Jade?'

'They just left.' I kept looking down at the cards. I couldn't even begin to try to explain any of this. Especially not to Beth.

'Oh. Well, how did it go?' she asked. 'Did you have a good time?' Her eyes beamed hopefully, because of course what she actually meant was: *Did you remember anything? Anything at all? Pretty please?*

'Yeah, it was great,' I said. 'They were both really nice.' I turned over the nine of hearts. Even to me, my voice did not exactly sound enthusiastic.

'Well, did you—?' Beth stopped, clamping her mouth shut. Finally she turned the kettle on and smiled thinly at me. 'Good,' she said. 'I'm glad.'

Chapter Ten

Kathy

6 February

The last thing I wanted to do was go to school today and hear all about the wonderful party at Tina's, but Mum said if I didn't go back I'd have to see the doctor today, so I went. I SO wish that I had gone to the doctor's instead. The absolute worst thing has happened – Poppy, Jade and Tina saw me in town on Saturday! I never even noticed them.

Jade came up to me first thing this morning and said, 'I knew you were faking.' So of course I told her that I hadn't been and asked what she meant, and she said, 'We SAW you, OK?' It turns out that they all went to see a film Saturday afternoon, and saw me when they passed by Debenham's, when I was in there looking at a jacket.

I tried to explain that the virus had only been a twenty-four hour thing, and that I really *had* been ill on Friday. I told her she could ask my mum if she didn't believe me. Poppy had come over too by then, and she and Jade just looked at me and didn't say a word. I pulled my phone out and said, 'Go on, then, ring her!'

Jade said I was being pathetic, and that OF COURSE she wasn't going to ring my mother! I told her to stop acting like a private detective, then, and she got really arsey and said she'd had enough of me being all stroppy and weird for no reason. She said I had really changed, ever since Richard moved in, and it was like I was taking it all out on Tina.

'Why *do* you hate Tina so much?' asked Poppy. 'We just really don't get it.'

'I DON'T hate Tina!' I said. 'I was ill!' We went back and forth for ages. I could tell they didn't believe me in the slightest. God, it's so unfair! Why is it such a crime not to like Tina? Is she like a goddess or something, that we all have to bow down and worship her?

Finally Jade said that she thought I was totally lying, and that I hadn't gone to Tina's because I was jealous of her. Jealous! That is just so ridiculous! I mean, of WHAT? Her ginger hair? Her so-called violin playing? Her pony-tailed dad who looks like an utter hippy reject?

I said that to them, and Poppy blew out her breath and said, 'Oh, *Kathy*,' in this really impatient tone. The bell went then, and the two of them walked off together. Before they did, Jade said that Tina thought I hated her, and that she was probably going to ask Mrs Boucher for a different FAB buddy.

That would seriously be all I need right now, for Mrs Boucher to ring up Mum and tell her that Tina wants a different FAB buddy, because I'm being so horrible to her! So when the bell went for break, I grabbed Tina before Poppy and Jade could latch onto her, and tried to explain about being ill. Plus I told her I was gutted that I missed her party, and that I would absolutely love to come round to her house, anytime she said.

She seemed sort of wary of me at first, but finally she smiled and said, 'Yeah, I've done that before too – thought I felt better than I actually did.'

'I'm really sorry,' I told her again, and she said it was OK, but that it was too bad I had missed the party. She started telling me about it, and I'm so incredibly glad I didn't go – it sounds like all they did was hang out with her perfect dad and mess around on the violin. I kept smiling, though, and pretended I could hardly wait to go over there myself.

Then Poppy and Jade came over in the middle of Tina telling me about it, and Jade said, 'So, are you two all made up, then?' Which I thought was SO cheeky of her, but Tina just laughed and said, 'Yeah, no probs.'

So now I guess I have to go over to Tina's house. Please, God, let her forget about inviting me!

8 February

I tried to talk to Mum tonight. I should have *known* it would be a massive mistake! But Richard had to work late, so Mum made tea for a change, and it was just the two of us, like it used to be. I mean, it's not like we always got on even then, but we got on about a million times better than we have been lately.

She asked me how school was going, and I told her about my science project, and the history paper I just got back (another C, argh – didn't tell her that part). I don't know – we were just getting on really well, so for some daft reason I thought maybe I could talk to her about Dad.

I wasn't sure how to put it, though. Finally I just said that I wished I could have seen Dad again. She said that she wished I could have too, and I said, 'But I could have, only you didn't let me.'

I wasn't trying to get at her, I really, honestly wasn't! I guess – this is so stupid – I guess I just wanted her to say sorry. Or something. But instead she started talking about how difficult the divorce was, on and on, until finally she said there were things I didn't know about that had affected her decision at the time.

'Like what?' I asked, but she wouldn't tell me. So I said, 'Oh, right, I bet there wasn't even a reason at all!'

I could tell she was trying to be calm and understanding, but she still said she couldn't tell me and that I just needed to trust her. Trust her, right. I pointed out that she let Richard move in, even though she knew I didn't want him to, so why exactly should I trust her? Which didn't go down too well – understatement! It ended up with both of us shouting at each other, and her calling me selfish again. Finally she sent me to my room. I banged the door so hard that a bit of plaster chipped off the wall. Good!

IT IS SO UNFAIR!! He was my father – why won't she tell me what happened? If there really *is* some mysterious reason, which I doubt. Personally, I think she was angry with him over the divorce, because I know he didn't want to give her as much money as she wanted. It's like she put a price tag on me, and wouldn't let him see me until he coughed up!

Later

I feel so sad now. I keep remembering all these things about Dad. Like, how scared we used to be of him sometimes, the two of us tiptoeing around the house like little mice. And how he used to smack her. He didn't do it that often, but it was so incredibly awful whenever it happened.

I didn't get a chance to say any of that to Mum. I don't BLAME her for leaving him, OK? I just wanted to see him again, that's all! Yes, I know he wasn't very nice sometimes, but he was my *dad.* Besides, sometimes he was fantastic. He honestly was. Like when he gave me Cat. And I know for a fact that Cat was really expensive, so that obviously proves that he loved me, right?

I just heard Richard come in. He and Mum are talking downstairs now, whispering away. I hate it that Mum is even talking to him about this! He's nothing to do with me!

9 February

Mum said she's 'sorry we lost our tempers with each other'. Whatever.

Happy face at school, as usual. Tra la la.

10 February

Jade's getting all excited about Valentine's Day, because she's madly in love with this Year Ten boy called Ian Lindley. She's planning on sending loads of cards to him, all signed 'Guess who?' I guess if he guesses right, he gets her for a Valentine's Day present.

Tina's still going on and on about her dad, violin, etc., etc. What else is new? She's such a broken record, even if Poppy and Jade can't see it for some weird reason. In fact, Poppy was saying today that she wants to have a sleepover at her house soon, for the four of us.

I might actually go to that if she does. It's just her and her mum, and no violin in sight!

13 February

NOOO!!! Tina's asked me to sleep over at her house on Friday night! Just me this time, without even Poppy and Jade along. I tried to make an excuse, but it was after school and her dad was *right there*, picking her up. He said, 'Oh, come on, it'll be fun. Though mind you, the house still hasn't recovered yet from Poppy and Jade coming round.'

I almost said I'd have to ask Mum, but I was afraid he'd ring her right then and there. And Tina was standing there smiling at me, and that was it, I was trapped.

So I had to say yes.

14 February

Tina keeps talking to me about what DVDs I want to

rent, and whether I like pepperoni or pineapple or both on my pizza. She really seems excited that I'm coming round. I'm supposed to bring my overnight bag with me to school tomorrow, and then go home with her and her dad. I feel like my face is about to crack from all the smiling I've been doing.

God, *why* did I say I'd go?? When I asked Mum about it I tried to sound completely unenthusiastic, so she'd say no, but she said, 'Of course, that sounds like fun.' And looked really pleased. I bet Jade's right. She's probably already planning on buying candles and wine for a romantic dinner for two, for her and her *live-in lover.*

He brought home a bunch of flowers for Mum tonight that made mine look completely puny. Plus they gave each other valentine cards, staring all mushily at each other, and then after tea I caught them kissing in the kitchen. A real kiss, not just a peck on the lips. I mean, they had their arms around each other and were using tongues and everything.

It made me feel sick, seeing Mum like that. I backed straight out again, not saying anything, and then later Richard came into the lounge to get something and asked if Cupid had been good to me today. Meaning did I get any cards.

I told him it wasn't any of his business, and went upstairs and banged my door shut. Mum didn't come up, so I guess she's too busy snogging lover-boy to bother.

Ian Lindley didn't guess, by the way. Jade says she doesn't like him that much anyway.

17 February

I didn't spend the night at Tina's after all. I don't want to talk about it.

Later

It's after 1.00 a.m. and I can't stop crying. I'm doing it really quietly, so that Mum and Richard won't hear, but I just can't stop.

I can't believe I did that. I wish I could just sink into the ground and disappear forever. I acted like such an IDIOT, and Tina's going to tell everyone, I just know it. *Everyone* will know.

I wish I could die.

Chapter Eleven

Kat

After tea that night, I told Richard and Beth I was tired and went up the stairs to my room, my fingers trailing on the banister. What was I going to do? If Jade were telling the truth, then that group of girls might have done something awful to me. I had to find out, but how? They weren't about to tell me, that was obvious enough.

I opened the door to my room, and blinked. Lying on my bed was a CD, still in its plastic wrapping. I picked it up. *Mahler, Symphony No. 5.* Richard!

Thoughts of Jade flew completely out of my head. Clutching the CD, I dashed downstairs again, grinning so widely that I could feel my cheeks stretching.

'Richard! Thank you!'

He and Beth were sitting on the sofa talking, but they broke off when I burst into the lounge. Richard smiled. 'Oh, you found it, then.'

'Yes! Thank you! It's perfect!' Without thinking, I swooped down and gave him a hug.

A startled laugh burst out from him, and he hugged me back with one arm. 'Glad you like it.'

'I'm going to go and play it right now.' I smiled down at the CD, turning it over in my hand. There was a painting of the sea on the front cover, with *Royal Philharmonic Orchestra* written below it.

Beth cleared her throat. 'It'll be nice to hear classical music in the house again.'

I looked up quickly. 'Did I used to play classical music, then?' I asked.

'Sometimes,' said Beth. 'You didn't like all of it, but some of it you really loved. Mahler is a new one, though. I think.'

'What else did I like?' I said faintly, holding the CD.

'Oh, let me think . . . Mozart. Brahms. Bach, you loved Bach. You used to play one of his violin concertos all the time.'

'Well – why did I stop listening to it?' The words burst out of me.

Beth shook her head. 'I don't know. I hadn't really thought about it until now.' An awkward silence fell around us. Suddenly I wondered if I should have hugged her as well. Were her feelings hurt that I hadn't? I hesitated, but my arms were frozen to my sides. I just couldn't do it; it would be like lying.

I backed away a step. 'Well – thanks again,' I said to Richard.

He grinned and lifted his hand in a half-salute. 'Any time.'

The music was as wonderful as I remembered. It started slow, with a single trumpet blowing, and then built and built until it was a whirlwind of sound, like a storm crashing through a forest. I sat cross-legged on the bed with my eyes shut tightly, letting it wash over me and sweep me away.

Finally the CD ended, and I slowly opened my eyes, hugging my knees to my chest. I let out a breath, looking around my room.

It was actually starting to feel like my room now, even though it still didn't have much to do with anything I liked. For instance, I hated the posters of actors and pop stars all over the walls – it was like being stared at by a bunch of grinning strangers. Most of them were of a boy with wavy dark hair and brooding eyes. Beth had told me that he was called Orlando Bloom, and that I had really, really liked him. Apparently I had seen some film called *Pirates of the Caribbean* four times.

Now I stared at the poster of Orlando over the desk, thinking about what I had been like when I was Kathy.

Maybe I had more in common with my old self than I had thought. Would I have liked Mahler's Fifth Symphony? If the old me were here now, what would she think of it? For a moment I imagined her opening the bedroom door and coming into the room, separate from me, smiling.

'What happened?' I whispered. *Why* had I been so afraid of Jade and the others?

I jumped up and hit 'play' on the CD player. As the symphony began again, I started opening up drawers and pawing through them. There had to be something in here that would tell me what had been going on, what I had really been like! Why Jade and Poppy, supposedly my best friends, hated me now.

But there was nothing. I looked through all the drawers, and even searched through the book bag I had been carrying when the car hit me, which the woman driving it had found and given back to Beth. That felt spooky, like going through things belonging to a ghost.

All it had in it were textbooks and exercise books, though. I flipped through them. I had had loopy, precise handwriting, and obviously hadn't liked history very much, if the amount of doodles in the margin had anything to do with it.

I sat back on my heels, blowing out a heavy breath. The music had turned soft and gentle, like a summertime breeze off a lake. 'Kathy, where are you?' I murmured. 'Come on, help me out. Where are you hiding?'

My gaze drifted to the bed. It was a single that sat pressed against the wall, with a white reading light attached to the headboard. Hang on – I sat up straighter, thinking. *Hiding.* If I were going to hide something – I mean, if there were something that really mattered to me – I wouldn't put it in one of my drawers or my school bag. I'd really hide it.

A moment later, I was gently scooting the bed out from the wall. Flopping down onto my stomach, I worked my hand under the mattress, running it along the length of the bed. Nothing there. I frowned and tried again, worming my hand as far under the mattress as I could. My palm tingled as I swept it along.

Suddenly my heart leaped. I was touching the tip of something smooth and hard. My fingers strained for it, nudging it towards me, and then my hand closed around it, and I pulled it out.

A small stone statue of a cat nestled in my hand. It stared up at me with an inscrutable expression, almost smiling. A tiny hoop earring ran through one of its ears, like a pirate cat.

I gazed down at it in wonder, running a finger down its snake-like spine. A cat. I had hidden a *cat.* And now I was called Kat. It seemed too bizarre to be a coincidence. Like the old part of me that was hidden was reaching out to me, asking for help.

I swallowed, tightening my fingers around the statue. 'I'll help you,' I whispered. 'I'll find out what happened.'

Nobody had mentioned my going to school yet, and after what had happened that afternoon with Poppy and Jade it was pretty much the last place on the planet that I wanted to go. But I knew now that I had to. Because if *they* knew what had happened to me, then other people might too.

And I had to find out.

I saw the hard look in Jade's dark eyes again, and shivered. '*You* knew, I bet,' I murmured to the cat. 'I wish you could just tell me.'

He gazed up at me, as unmoving as if he had lain hidden for a thousand years.

* * *

Beth looked very relieved when I mentioned going back to school to her the next morning. She leaned against the kitchen worktop, holding a cup of coffee.

'Yes, brilliant idea – I would have suggested it myself in a few more days. We were just waiting for you to feel up to it, but I think it would really help you get your memory back.'

My memory again. My lips tightened with the effort to hold in a groan. Why did she *always* have to bang on about it?

Amazingly, Beth grimaced. She put her cup on the counter. 'Sorry, there I go again,' she said. 'I know I keep pushing about your memory. I don't mean to.' She tried to smile.

Well, you do a pretty good job of it for someone who doesn't even mean to, I thought. I didn't say it.

She sighed, gazing out at the garden. A neighbour's cat was prowling through it like he owned it – a fluffy white and brown creature with a plume-like tail. Beth took a breath. 'It's just – well, I guess I miss you.'

I shrugged stiffly. 'I'm still here, even if I don't remember anything.'

'I know, but—' Beth broke off, and quickly poured herself some more coffee. 'Never mind. You're right,' she said, stirring in a dollop of milk. She looked up and smiled. Her face looked stretched, uncomfortable.

'Look, why don't I ring your headmistress today and see what she suggests? How much do you remember from your lessons?'

Part of me wanted to slam out of the room without even answering – let her wait forever for her *real* daughter to come back. Instead I put my hand in my pocket, feeling the stone weight of the cat nestled there. He gave me courage, and I took a deep breath.

'Not that much,' I admitted. 'I was looking through the textbooks last night . . . I think I could catch up pretty quickly, though.'

Beth nodded. 'And school's definitely the right place for you. You need to be back with your friends, don't you?'

Friends. I tried to smile. 'Yeah, definitely.'

Dr Perrin's office didn't feel any more inviting the second time I was in it. I sat on the same saggy green sofa as before, and spent the whole forty-five minutes putting my hand to my mouth and then snatching it away again. My nails were starting to grow out a bit, and I was trying to stop biting them.

Dr Perrin read through my dream journal with her eyes narrowed, nodding slightly to herself. 'Very interesting, Kat. Now, this dream you had on Thursday night, where you were hiking up a tall mountain in the snow – how did you feel during it? What was the prevailing *mood* of the dream?'

I put on a thoughtful face, like I was trying really, really hard to remember. Actually, I had forgotten to write down my dreams a couple of mornings, so I'd scribbled down a bunch of pretend dreams an hour ago, using different pens so she wouldn't catch me out.

'Um . . . I felt OK,' I told her.

One of her painted eyebrows lifted slightly. 'No feelings of tension or stress?'

Wrong answer, obviously. I pretended to think about it. 'Well . . . maybe a little, because of all the snow – I was trudging through it, and it kept snowing, and I wasn't sure I could keep my footing.'

Dr Perrin's pen scratched across her notepad. I watched, fascinated with the way her hair stayed completely in place when she moved, with not even a single strand shifting.

She looked up, flashing her teeth at me. 'Well, that's very typical. And was there any sense of panic, like you *had* to get to the top of the mountain before something bad happened?'

I almost started laughing, and had to bite the inside of my cheek. 'Um . . . maybe a bit of panic.'

Her big toothy smile drooped at the edges. 'Just a bit?'

I rubbed my thumb. 'Maybe more than a bit.'

'Ah, now we're getting somewhere.' *Scribble, scribble.* 'Kat, it's very important that you note down *moods* in your dreams, as accurately as you can remember them.'

I nodded, making a mental note to myself to include fake feelings in my fake dreams from now on.

'Now then,' said Dr Perrin, 'obviously the sense of tension and panic in the dream relates to what's happening to you now, while the mountain represents the obstacles you're facing. Do you see? You feel that there's a mammoth task ahead of you, you're frightened that you'll fail, you wonder if you'll ever succeed at it.'

I went cold as she spoke. I tried not to let my face

show anything, but inside, my heart started pounding like one of the drums on Kathy's CDs. It was just a made-up dream! How did she *know* all that?

'Yes? Is that right?' asked Dr Perrin.

I felt my face go red. I lifted a shoulder, not looking at her. 'I guess.'

'Of course. It's a very fraught time for you, isn't it? Now, how's everything at home? Are you finding things less strange now?'

'I'm getting ready to go back to school,' I blurted out.

'Oh?' She wrote something down. 'And how do you feel about that?'

I stared at her pen, watching it move across the page. 'I . . . well, I guess sort of what you said. Like – like I'm not sure I'll succeed.' I took a deep breath, wondering if I should tell her about Poppy and Jade, and how strange they were acting.

Before I could decide, Dr Perrin put down her pen and beamed at me. 'Shall we work out some visualizations for you?'

Eh? I stared at her. 'Work out what?'

'Visualizations. A coping technique where you *see* yourself succeeding. Right, now I want you to picture yourself walking up the front steps of the school – try to see it really, really vividly. Now you're going into the building . . . Picture yourself making lots of friends and doing well . . .'

She went on and on like that, constructing this happy fake reality, when all I had wanted was to talk about how scared I was. She had this way of crinkling up the corners of her eyes when she smiled, like she thought it made her look more sincere or something. God, why had I told her *anything*?

I went back to staring at the clock.

My year head was called Mrs Boucher. Beth rang her up and they had a long chat, and then the next thing I knew I was at the school sitting in an empty classroom, doing a series of tests so that they could figure out what to do with me.

I didn't recognize anything about the school, not a single door or corridor. I bent over my test papers, trying to concentrate even though I knew Jade and Poppy were somewhere in the building. I was just glad I hadn't seen them.

That night Beth talked to Mrs Boucher again, and when she hung up the phone she looked pleased. 'She said she thinks you'll only need special help in maths and science, and that you should be able to go back into your old classes for everything else, so long as you have support.'

I was sitting at the table in the breakfast nook, practising Richard's card trick, working on the sleight of hand over and over. Sometimes I thought I just about had it, and then I'd drop the whole deck or something, and have to start again.

Now I stared down at the queen of clubs. 'That's great,' I said. Slowly, I shuffled the deck again, tapping the cards together and watching the bright reds and blacks merge together.

'She thinks that a FAB buddy would be a good idea

too,' Beth said, slicing up a green pepper. She was cooking tea for a change, since Richard had to work late.

The cut on my forehead gave a tiny throb as I frowned. 'A what buddy?'

Beth kept her eyes on the pepper, like it was taking all of her concentration to chop it. 'It's this programme called Friends and Buddies. You were part of it before your accident . . .' There was a pause, and then she cleared her throat and smiled at me.

'You helped out a new girl called Tina McNutt. So Mrs Boucher has asked Tina if she'd like to return the favour.'

Tina. My muscles tensed. 'What did she say?'

'She'd love to. She's going to meet you outside the front gates on Monday.'

So Tina didn't hate me! My heart flew up at the news. I did the sleight of hand perfectly, and grinned to myself. Thank God – I'd have one friend, at least.

Chapter Twelve

Kathy

18 February

Mum just came in, asking me what's wrong. *Again.* I wanted to say, What's wrong is that you won't leave me alone! Instead I told her that I'm fine, and Tina and I just had a row, that's all. Which is what I told her when I came home last night, no doubt ruining her romantic evening with Richard.

She kept trying for a bit, and then finally she said, 'Well, if you want to talk about it . . .' and left.

I am never, ever, going to want to talk about it.

19 February

Mum just asked if I wanted to go for a swim with her. She doesn't even like swimming that much, so I think she was trying to lure me out of my room, since I've hardly come out since I got home. But there was no way I could go to the pool with her – what if Poppy was there?! She'd be sure to ask how Friday night went.

If she doesn't know already. Oh God. I feel so ill, just thinking about it.

I'm going to write about it. Maybe it will help.

The bizarre thing is, when I first got to Tina's house I thought it might all be OK. She and her dad live in this tiny three-up, three-down. That surprised me, because somehow I thought it would be somewhere really lavish – though I'm not sure why I thought that when Mr McNutt's car is falling to bits.

We ordered pizza, and messed around for a bit. Finally we went up to Tina's room, which is almost as small as mine, with this huge mural of the sea on one wall – the one her dad painted, obviously. It was OK, I guess. Not *that* great. The main thing I noticed was that she had a music stand in the corner. I could see her violin case sitting next to it.

I don't know why I did this. I really don't. But I said, 'Why don't you play something?'

And Tina said OK, and got out her violin. She wasn't self-conscious at all. She started playing this piece she said she had been practising, and I knew it straight away – it was Mozart's Ave Verum. I played it to get my grade four, years ago. I always liked playing it, because it's basically this light, gentle piece, like walking through a forest. That sounds *so* soppy, but it's true.

Anyway, I listened to Tina play, and she was OK, I guess. A bit wobbly, maybe, and I couldn't *believe* that her teacher hadn't told her off about the angle that she was holding her bow. But she was OK. And the music was OK. It was sort of nice, in fact, sitting there and listening to her, and I started to relax about being there.

But then Tina stopped playing, and said, 'Hang on, you play the violin too, don't you?'

I thought I was going to faint, because I couldn't imagine *how* she knew that. But then she pointed with her bow and said that my hand had been moving, like I was playing.

I could have just lied to her – God, why didn't I?? But instead, for some *stupid* reason, I admitted that yeah, I used to play. And she said, 'Hey, do you want to play now? Here, have a go!'

I didn't want to, not really. The violin isn't me any more, and I don't want it to be. That person was such a total sap. She got hurt. Like, all the time. But at the same time, part of me *did* want to. So, I took the violin from her, and I played Mozart's Ave Verum.

I was pretty rusty at first, and I didn't have calluses any more, so the strings really hurt my fingers. But the music came for me, just like it always did, and after a few minutes it got smoother and stronger. I just played and played. I never wanted to stop.

When I finally did, Tina started going on about how fantastic I was, and WHY wasn't I in Band, and so on. And here's the really embarrassing part, the part that makes me want to just curl up and die. I couldn't let go of Tina's violin. I knew I should give it back to her, but I just couldn't.

And then I asked her if I could borrow it. WHY DID I SAY THAT??? WHY? And I couldn't just leave it there, even when I could see from her face that the answer was NO, because what else would it be – no, *then* I started going on about how I'd take really good care of it, and that I wouldn't keep it for long. I was practically *begging* her.

Tina looked really uncomfortable, and said she'd have to ask her dad, and suddenly I realized how pathetic and stupid I obviously seemed. I shoved her violin back at her and told her I didn't want to borrow it anyway. I said I was just joking, that actually I wouldn't borrow her violin if my life depended on it, because playing the violin was utterly naff and stupid, which was why I'd stopped.

Tina just stared at me like I had completely lost it. I guess maybe I had. That was when I called her a geek and said she made me sick. And then I grabbed my bag and ran out of their house.

I walked all the way home. I thought I was going to be ill once or twice on the way, but I wasn't. It took me hours, and when I finally, finally got home, there was this horrible scene because Mr McNutt had apparently been driving around looking for me, and had rung Mum – God.

I don't even want to go into all that, I'm too tired. It wasn't very nice, that's all. I got shouted at loads, for what felt like hours, and it was actually Richard, of all people, who got Mum to calm down and told me to go to bed.

Maybe I'll be ill again tomorrow. I can't go to school, I can't face seeing Tina. And Jade and Poppy – she's sure to tell them all about this! I feel so sick. Like I really *am* ill, in fact.

Later

Richard just came in, wanting to teach me one of his card tricks. He shuffled the deck and said, 'It's good therapy when you don't feel well. How about it?'

I told him I was too tired.

20 February

Thank God! Mum went to some sort of life-coaching conference in Reading today, so instead of going to school I went to the park until I knew they'd both be gone, and then came back home again. It feels so weird being home alone. I'm watching TV, but I can't relax. I'm afraid Mum or Richard might come back any second.

The school rang a while ago to see where I was. I let it go onto the answer phone and then erased the message. I know I'm just putting it off and that I'll probably have to go back tomorrow, but I can't help it. There is no way that I could have faced Tina today, or Jade, or ANYONE.

10.20 came and went, but no text from Jade. I bet Tina's told them everything by now. What are they saying about me??!

Later

I've been sleeping with Cat under my pillow – how sad is that? Like I need a security blanket or something. But I do need him. I need to be able to reach under my pillow and know that he's there. It's the only thing that even makes me feel halfway OK.

21 February
Mum was home today, so I had to go back. It was even worse than I thought it would be. The minute I got to school, I saw Poppy and Jade standing outside with Tina, the three of them in a huddle, whispering away. Then Poppy saw me, and she and Jade came right over, wanting to know what happened, and why I left Tina's house. I was right, Tina told them everything! I just shrugged and said, 'I was sick of Tina showing off, that's all.'

'But *you* were the one playing the violin,' said Jade. Then she wanted to know how come I never told them I could. I said it was no big deal, that *anyone* could play better than Tina.

Jade stared at me for a long time. Finally she said, 'You've really turned into a bitch, Kathy.' And she turned and walked away. She went back to Tina (who had been standing watching us) and the two of them started whispering. Tina looked really upset, but Jade just kept glaring at me, her eyes all narrow and hard.

Poppy said, 'Kathy, I don't understand. You used to be so nice! Now all you do is snarl at everyone and hate the world.'

I thought I was going to cry, so I told her to just leave me alone, she could think whatever she wanted to and I DIDN'T CARE. So she went over to Jade and Tina, and then the three of them stuck together all day long, talking about me. I know they were talking about me because they kept staring at me, and to make it even worse they've told Susan and Gemma and all the others about it too. I spent most of the day with my head down, trying to ignore everyone.

I hate Tina, I really do. Everything was completely fine before she moved here! And Poppy and Jade – I can't believe it. I mean, in a strange way I can't really blame *Tina* for telling everyone, because she hardly knows me and I acted like a nutter. But Poppy and Jade have known me for TWO YEARS! How can they turn against me like this?? And turn everyone else against me too? I thought they were my friends. I thought we'd be friends forever!

Mum just came in, wanting to know if I wanted to talk. I seemed depressed, she said. Oh really, what gave you that impression?! I told her everything was fine. Maybe I would have wanted to talk to her pre-Richard, but these days it's obvious that she cares more about him than me.

I still can't believe that she won't tell me whatever it is about Dad, and why she wouldn't let me see him after we left.

22 February

I hate going to school now, I just hate it. Everyone's talking about what happened at Tina's house. Gemma made this motion when she passed me in the corridor today, like she was playing a violin, and then Clare said, 'Ooh, can I *borrow* it?' and they both smirked at me, really nastily. I pretended I hadn't heard them, but inside me it felt like something was about to explode. The cows! And Poppy and Jade too. You'd think we'd never been friends at all, the way they're acting.

I sit on my own at lunch now. Tina sits where I used to sit. We always sit at the same table in the canteen whenever we can grab it, over by the windows, and now she sits in between Poppy and Jade, just like I used to. They've both been making a big fuss over her, glaring at me whenever they see me. Even Poppy.

Tina should just get over it! OK, I shouldn't have called her names and left her house, but here's a news flash: IT WASN'T THE END OF THE WORLD. Everyone's acting like I tried to poison her or something.

I should do something *really* horrible to her, then they'd see that it wasn't all that bad.

Chapter Thirteen

Kat

I stood in front of the school gate, feeling as conspicuous as a cold sore as everyone streamed past me. I shifted the book bag on my shoulder, watching down the pavement for Tina. Had I got it wrong? Maybe I was supposed to meet her *inside* the school.

Just as I was about to go into the building to check, I saw a short girl with ginger plaits walking towards me. She didn't seem in much of a hurry, even though we were practically late.

Then she got closer, and I caught my breath. Ginger plaits. It was the girl Jade had put her arm around after I got hit by the car. She was one of the ones I had been running away from!

When the girl reached me, she stopped, but she didn't say anything. She just sort of glanced at me, tightening her grip on the strap of her bag.

I swallowed. 'Um – are you Tina?'

Her cheeks coloured. 'We'd better go in. We're going to be late.'

She walked with her head down as we crossed the courtyard, gazing at her feet. The silence felt like a living thing trying to smother us. 'You were there, weren't you?' I blurted out.

She gave me a nervous glance. 'What do you mean?'

'When I was hit by the car. You were there with Jade.'

We were climbing the front steps by then. Tina was carrying a crocheted bag with a purple flower over one shoulder, and suddenly she started to run, the bag bouncing up and down at her side. She vanished into the building, not even waiting to see if I was following.

When I caught up with her, she was hurrying down the echoing corridor, staring straight ahead. 'Your first class is maths,' she said. 'I'm supposed to show you where it is.'

I got the hint.

Once I got to maths, I didn't have time to think about Tina any more, or Jade, or anything at all apart from trying not to look painfully stupid.

'Does everyone understand about long division now?' asked Mrs Farnham, the maths teacher. She scanned the class, tapping a marker against her palm. There were only about fifteen of us, and everyone else was nodding, looking bored.

She smiled at me. 'Kat? How about you?'

I bit my lip as everyone glanced at me. My head was still swimming with decimal points and numbers columns.

A boy with black hair and pimples groaned. 'Can't

we get on with it, Miss?' I winced. Nobody knew I had amnesia in this class; they all just thought I was a really thick new girl with a red scar across her forehead. At least the stitches had finally come out. Not that that made me feel any better just then.

'We'll be moving on to something else soon, Tom.' Mrs Farnham handed out worksheets for everyone to do on their own, and then came and crouched down beside me. 'Let's go through a few of these together, Kat – everyone else has had a whole week of long division already.'

I felt a bit less thick when she said that, but it was still hard. Mrs Farnham whispered instructions as I struggled to understand, my numbers scrawling across the page. 'No, no – remember, you need to count over and find the decimal point . . .'

My fingers tightened on the pencil as I rubbed out the last line of numbers, and I thought to Kathy, Thanks a bunch for taking maths with you, wherever you are.

English was even worse. Everyone knew exactly who I was.

The teacher wasn't there yet when we walked in, and at first everyone was chattering away, but then people saw me and fell still. Tina slid into a seat without looking at me.

I hesitated, feeling everyone watching. Finally I sat down beside her. The second I did, she moved her chair, sitting as far from me as possible without leaving the table. I felt like a disease that had just slimed its way into the room.

'Tina, do you want to sit with Poppy and me?' said someone loudly.

Jade. My head jerked up. She and Poppy were at a table in the corner. Jade stood up, tossing her head and pulling out an empty chair. 'There's plenty of room, if we just budge up a bit,' she announced.

My face caught fire. Everyone was watching, waiting to see what Tina would do. A boy with blond hair snickered. 'Ooh, cat fight, cat fight!'

'Yeah, *Kat* fight,' I heard someone else whisper. ' 'Cos she's changed her name now, hasn't she?'

Tina hesitated, pulling at one of her ginger plaits. 'That's OK,' she said finally.

Jade's dark eyes flashed. 'Come on, Tina. You don't want to sit with *her*.'

Before Tina could answer, the door opened and a thin woman with curly brown hair rushed in. 'Sorry, sorry – I had to stop and talk to someone. Take your seats, everyone.'

Jade slowly sat down, sending a hard stare in my direction.

'Kathy! Oh, sorry, I mean Kat – good to see you back.' The woman put a pile of papers down on her desk and smiled at me.

The stares felt like my skin was on fire. 'Thanks,' I said.

I sat hiding in the loo at break, biting my newly grown nails and shouting at myself for being such a coward. This was *not* the way to find out what had happened! But every time I told myself to get out there, find Jade and the others, and demand to know the truth, I remembered the whole class staring at me, and I just couldn't do it.

On the inside of the loo door, someone had written: *Maddy & Paul, True Luv 4 EVA!!* Great. At least someone was happy.

I opened up my book bag and pulled out a small object wrapped in a handkerchief. Holding it on my lap, I unfolded the thin white cloth until finally the cat statue peeped out at me. I picked him up, and he seemed to gaze at me with a tiny smile on his feline face. Like he was saying, 'Come on, cheer up – it can't be *that* bad, can it?'

I didn't know. Maybe it could. I traced the curve of his tail around his feet. 'Why did I run out into traffic?' I whispered. 'Why was I so scared of them?'

I jumped as the bell blared through the air. Hastily, I wrapped up the cat again, tucking him back in my bag. As I was picking it up, it hit me that he was another mystery.

Why had I hidden him away?

We had double history after break, but this time nobody said a word to me. Or to anyone else, for that matter. The teacher, Mr Chappell, had this really soft voice, but something about his eyes gave you the feeling that he might go berserk and throw the whiteboard at you if you stepped out of line. Which no one did. There wasn't a single whisper, not for the whole two hours.

When the bell rang, everyone jumped up,

grabbing their things. I stood up slowly, glancing at Tina. She hadn't looked at me once, even though we had sat together again.

'Um – it's time for lunch now, right?' I asked.

Bright red flowers blossomed on her cheeks. She stared down at her bag as she zipped it up, like she hated even hearing my voice.

Out of the corner of my eye, I could see Jade and Poppy weaving round the tables towards us, and I winced. No, hang on – I couldn't let them scare me like this! We were in the middle of a classroom; what could they do?

I turned towards them, squaring my shoulders and trying to look as if I wasn't nervous in the least. Poppy faltered a bit, her round face uncertain. Jade didn't look uncertain at all. Her eyebrows lowered, like she'd welcome the chance for a showdown.

'Kat, could I see you for a moment?' called Mr Chappell from the front of the room.

I tried not to show how utterly relieved I was as I went up to his desk. He peered at me through his wire-rimmed glasses. 'How are you doing? Are you remembering anything at all?'

'No, not really.' My neck felt warm; I was *so* aware of Poppy, Jade and Tina standing just a few metres away, probably listening to every word.

He smiled. 'Well, I shan't take the fact that you've forgotten my lessons personally. Right, well, this stuff about the Romans probably isn't making much sense to you at the moment, but— Hold on there, you girls,' he called suddenly, glancing towards the door.

Jade, Poppy and Tina froze, looking over their shoulders at him.

'Tina, aren't you Kat's FAB partner?'

Tina gulped, her cheeks suddenly matching her hair. 'Yes, sir.'

Mr Chappell shook his head, tapping a pen on his desk. 'Well, then wait a minute, can't you? You'll need to show Kat where the canteen is when I'm through with her.'

Tina whispered something to Jade and Poppy. The two of them left slowly, glancing back at me. My stomach dipped. They did not look friendly.

'Right,' said Mr Chappell. 'As I was saying, if you'll just bear with us for a week or so, then we're going to start studying the Aztecs, and you'll be on the same footing as everyone else. Meanwhile, if you need any help, just give me a yell. All right?'

I nodded. I could feel Tina standing in the doorway, watching me. 'All right,' I said.

We walked to the canteen in utter silence. Sentences kept forming in my head, like: *Thanks so much for waiting, it was really great of you,* and *You're not very talkative, are you?* Tina paced along beside me, staring straight ahead, her ginger plaits hanging down her back.

I smelled the canteen before we got there – the scent of spag bol and chips hung heavily in the air. Tina and I queued in silence. What a surprise. I slid my tray along and got a sandwich and a salad. The spag bol was shiny with grease, but Tina didn't seem to notice. She carefully perched a bit of garlic bread beside hers.

By the time we sat down at a table, I couldn't take it any more. 'Look,' I said, unwrapping my sandwich. 'Can't you tell me why you and the others hate me so much? Please?'

Tina darted a glance at me. 'I think you know, actually.'

'I don't!' I leaned towards her. 'Please, tell me – was I really friends with Poppy and Jade? Why was I *scared* of them?'

'You shouldn't stand for this, Tina,' said a loud voice behind us.

I whipped round in my seat. Jade was standing there with Poppy. She flipped her long hair back. 'Tina, you should go talk to Mrs Boucher. There is *no way* that you should have to be Kathy's FAB partner!'

I met Jade's eyes, trying not to let my voice shake. 'Why shouldn't she be, though? I was hers, wasn't I?'

Tina gasped, looking like I had slapped her. Poppy hurried over beside her and squeezed her shoulder. 'That was really low, even for you,' she said to me.

I shook my head, close to tears. 'I don't understand—'

'It's just what she's like, though, isn't it?' said Jade coldly. 'Tina, come on, you don't want to sit here.'

Tina stared down at her spag bol. 'Jade, just leave it,' she said softly. 'Please.'

Jade looked like she wanted to argue some more, but then she let out a breath and took Poppy's arm. 'Fine. But Tina, I seriously think you should come with us. You should *not* have to put up with being with *her*!'

After they had left, Tina and I sat in silence for a long time. She ate her spag bol slowly, staring down at her plate. I fiddled with the plastic container my sandwich had come in. 'You know, if you told me why you all hate me so much, then maybe—'

I jumped as Tina threw down her fork with a clatter. 'Leave me alone! OK? Haven't you done enough already?'

'But—'

'Just leave me alone!' Tina grabbed her bag and jumped up, knocking her tray sideways. Her garlic bread fell onto the floor. In a rush of ginger plaits, she was gone, hurrying across the canteen.

I sat there alone, feeling like I had just grown two heads. Finally I picked up my sandwich and took a bite. Limp ham and cheese. I put it back down again. It tasted like damp cardboard.

Just before the bell rang, Poppy appeared at my table. 'Tina doesn't want to be your FAB partner any more,' she announced. 'So I'm going to do it, so she doesn't get in trouble.'

I shoved the rest of my sandwich back into the plastic container. My hands were shaking. 'Why would she get in trouble, if I'm such a terrible person?'

'Because she said she'd do it,' said Poppy. 'But she just can't, and I don't blame her. I'll show you where your classes are from now on instead.'

The bell reverberated through the air. All at once the canteen came alive with chairs scraping back, and people streaming towards the bins to dump their rubbish.

'Why are you even bothering?' I stood up, grabbing my tray. 'You think I'm *faking* it, right?'

Poppy looked at me coldly. 'Yeah, but the teachers don't know that, do they?'

Beth picked me up again after school. Apparently I used to walk to school, but it was almost a mile and Beth was afraid I might get lost now. As I got into her car that afternoon, I thought that getting lost sounded like an excellent idea.

'How did it go?' asked Beth. Her face was alight, hopeful.

'Great.' With my good arm, I hefted my book bag onto the back seat and banged the door shut.

'Did you—?' She stopped short. 'I mean . . . how were your classes? Did Tina show you around?'

'Yeah, everything was fine.' I looked out of the window. Black-uniformed students everywhere, swarming out from the school in all directions. I thought I saw Jade, and almost slid down in my seat – but then I saw it was someone else, and felt like an idiot. Great, now I was getting jumpy on top of everything else.

Beth manoeuvred the car onto the main road. 'So you're glad you went back?'

I shrugged. 'Yeah, I guess.'

She blew out a breath. 'Kat . . . could you please just *talk* to me?'

'I am! I mean, sorry; there just isn't much to tell.'

Beth slowed down for a roundabout, craning her

neck as she watched the flow of traffic. 'You seem upset.'

I looked down at my coat, not answering. It was heavy and black, with black buttons and a black belt. And I had a black scarf around my neck. Suddenly the outfit felt like it was trying to smother me. 'I'm just . . . sick of these clothes!' I burst out.

Beth glanced at me in surprise. 'You're what?'

'These clothes! Everything I had before was black, or brown, or grey, and my *uniform* is black as well – I feel like a great black crow, flapping about!'

Beth started to laugh.

'What?' I asked sullenly, pulling off the scarf and throwing it onto the back seat.

'It's just – Kat, I've been saying for *years* that you should add a bit of colour to your wardrobe! Before your accident, I think the only time I ever saw you wearing that red top I gave you is when you first tried it on.'

'Yeah, well, you were right,' I muttered. I slumped back against the seat, scowling at the dashboard.

At the next roundabout, Beth turned the car round. I sat up. 'Where are we going?'

She smiled at me. 'How does a bit of retail therapy sound?'

Chapter Fourteen

Kathy

23 February

I sat with Rachel and Holly at lunch today. I don't think they've heard anything about what happened at Tina's; they're not really part of our group. That's because no one likes them, but I was desperate. I HATE eating alone – it looks beyond sad, like I have leprosy or something.

Rachel and Holly both have ponies, and apparently they get up at about 5.00 a.m. to ride them and brush them down and whatever. They kept going on and on about them at lunch, talking to each other like I wasn't even there. They weren't *ignoring* me, exactly, just too enthralled in the land of ponies to pay me any attention.

Tina's still acting like an utter martyr, with Poppy and Jade hovering around her like she's wasting away or something. (I wish!) Yes, poor Tina-Wina – someone called you names, ooh, how are you ever going to get over it? She doesn't even *know* what it's like to have bad things to get over – her with her perfect dad, who paints sea murals on her wall and plays midnight jam sessions with her!

She caught me glaring at her during break today, and she looked really startled, and then just miserable. Good! She seriously needs to grow up.

Richard tried to talk to me during tea tonight, asking how school was. For a change he didn't try to make any stupid jokes, but I still wasn't in the mood to have a conversation with him. He sort of smiled and said, 'Oh well, thought I'd try,' and then Mum gave me a dirty look.

I can't help it. Every time I sort of get used to him being here, I think about Dad, and then I just want him to go away. *Dad* was my family, and *Mum* is my family – Richard has nothing to do with it. Mum hasn't even been seeing him for a year yet!

I've been remembering so many things about Dad – the good stuff, for a change. The way he used to kiss me goodnight after reading me a bedtime story, his cheek all warm and scratchy against mine. 'Night, night,' he used to say. 'Don't let the bedbugs bite.' That scared me, about bedbugs, until Mum explained it was just a saying. There's loads of other stuff too. He could be so great, sometimes.

So why did he do that? *Why?* I keep thinking about it and thinking about it. It's never gone away, really. And he didn't even apologize, that was the worst thing. Well, not that he got a chance to, since Mum didn't let me see him after we left . . . but he could have written, or phoned, or something.

I hate thinking about this. I want to change the

subject, but there's nothing good to change it to. Everything's horrible.

Later

Oh no, I'm so embarrassed! I thought I was doing really well, and not acting like any of this is getting to me too much, but then tonight while I was taking a bath, I just started crying. I couldn't help it. Then as I was going back to my room Richard came upstairs, and he knew straight away that I had been crying – probably not hard to figure out, since my eyes were all damp and swollen!

I just wanted to die. He asked if everything was OK, and I said it was fine. He started to say something, but instead he just sort of nodded, and started to go past me to their bedroom. I blurted out, 'Don't tell Mum, OK?' And he smiled and said, 'I won't, don't worry. But do you want to talk about it? I'm very good at listening.'

As if! I shook my head and dashed back to my room. Now I'm waiting for Mum to come in any second now and demand to know what's up. So far she hasn't.

Maybe he really won't tell her.

24 February

I've done something terrible. I can't believe I did it. I didn't *plan* it, it just . . . sort of happened. And now I don't know what to do – it's too late to take it back, everyone would know!

What am I going to do with it?! Thank God it's still

wintertime, and no one's been near the shed for ages. I can't keep it there, though. I can't *keep* it at all! What have I done?

Later

I really am scared. What if someone finds out it was me?

Chapter Fifteen

Kat

Beth drove us to Festival Place, the big shopping centre in the middle of town. I had never seen it before, and my mouth dropped when I saw the glass multi-coloured tower reaching up into the sky. It looked like something from the future.

Inside was pretty impressive too. Shop after shop, each one more exciting than the last. Beth bought me new jeans and a bunch of new jumpers, all different colours, plus a bright red coat that I absolutely loved. I modelled it for her, putting the hood up and down.

'Oh, it really suits you, that colour,' said Beth. Then she laughed. 'I'll never lose you in a crowd now, will I?'

I smiled, looking at myself in the mirror. 'Definitely not,' I said.

Afterwards we went to a coffee shop outside Debenham's, balancing our mountain of shopping bags. Beth got me a cappuccino, and I spooned the froth off it. 'This is really good,' I said.

'Yes, you always used to like those.' And for the first time ever, she didn't sigh, or look sad – she just smiled, and stirred her coffee. 'This is nice, isn't it? We should do this more often.'

I nodded, swirling the chocolate powder around with my spoon and wondering if I could tell her what was happening at school. No, bad idea – she probably wouldn't even want me to go back if she knew, and how else could I find out what had happened to me?

There was something else I wanted to know about, though. Something only Beth could tell me. I started to speak, and stopped.

She put down her coffee, her eyes warm with concern. 'What is it?'

I stared down at the table, tracing the marble pattern with my finger. 'Um . . . I was just – wondering about my dad.'

Her eyebrows flew up. Suddenly she seemed to be holding the coffee cup like a shield in front of her. 'Your father?'

'Nana said that he was really charming.'

The side of Beth's mouth twisted wryly. 'She said that?'

I nodded, struggling to describe the look on Nana's face, the thread of hardness in her voice. 'Yeah, but . . . I wasn't sure that she meant it.'

Beth let out a breath, sagging back into her seat. 'Oh, he could be very charming, all right,' she said. 'He – Kat, the thing is, he – he had a lot of problems, really.'

What did *that* mean? I frowned. 'You mean like at work?'

'No – well, yes, I suppose he did; he was a bit of a

workaholic. But no, I meant—' Beth shoved her hair back with one hand. She seemed to be searching for the right words. 'He had a lot of problems when he was growing up,' she said finally. 'He was an abused child, I guess you'd call it. His father was – well . . . And, you know, not to make excuses for him, but that made him a difficult person sometimes. He—'

'Beth, hello!' A woman with streaky brown and blonde hair stopped at our table, carrying a tray with a coffee and a muffin on it. 'Sneaking in a bit of shopping, eh?'

Beth looked up, startled, and then laughed. 'Yes, that's right – oh dear, caught in the act! Kat, this is—'

I was still thinking about my dad; I had hardly even noticed the woman. But I glanced up at her and heard myself say, 'You're Beth's old boss, from when we first moved here.'

And then blinked, wondering where the words had come from.

Beth's head whipped about as she stared at me. Her lips turned pale.

'You remember her?' she whispered. She put her hand on my arm, but gently, like it was a butterfly she was afraid might fly away. 'Kat – you actually *remember* her?'

I shook my head, confused. I didn't remember anything; I just knew that this was Beth's old boss, somehow.

She looked as confused as I was. She glanced from Beth to me, and back again. Taking a step back, she said, 'Well . . . I'll leave you to finish your coffees. Nice to see you, Beth.'

I could feel Beth's eyes still on me as the woman walked off. She sat without moving a single muscle, just staring at me, as though she was hardly even breathing. It made my stomach feel tight and strange, so that when she cleared her throat and said, 'Shall we go home now?' I just nodded, and gathered up my bags.

We didn't go home, though. Halfway there, Beth turned left onto Roman Road. 'Listen, let's pop by Doctor Perrin's office first, shall we? We might just catch her before she goes home for the day.'

'What for?' My heart started pounding.

'Just to see.' Beth glanced at me. 'It's just that this could be hugely important, love – we need to get it checked out straight away.'

I chewed a nail. 'Get what checked out?'

'Kat! Your *memory*. You might be getting it back, don't you see?'

I slumped down in my seat, hating the excitement in her voice. It was like now that I might be *Kathy* again, I was a million times better than just Kat, and she could hardly wait to see. And I had thought we were getting on so well. I stared down at the shopping bags nestling at my feet, hating them suddenly.

It was even worse when we got to the hospital.

'No, I won't make an appointment!' Beth leaned towards the receptionist, gripping the edge of the counter. 'Listen, you don't understand, my daughter has amnesia – but today she actually remembered something, for the first time! It's *vital* that we get it checked out! Is Doctor Perrin here? Can't you just ring her?'

Beth got her way, and twenty minutes later I was sitting in Dr Perrin's office. Her honey-coloured hair looked even stiffer than normal, like a helmet clinging to her head. 'Hello, Kat. Your mother tells me that you've remembered something.'

I shrugged, hating the way her pen stood poised and ready over her notepad.

She flashed her shark-smile at me. 'Have you *not* remembered something?'

'I guess . . .' I told her what had happened, staring at the photo of the fairy-wing girl on the wall. 'But I don't know if it actually meant anything. Except to Beth,' I added bitterly.

She raised a pencilled eyebrow. 'Oh? Why is that?'

The words tore out of me. 'Because it's all she ever thinks about! *My memory* – have I remembered something, have I remembered something! She doesn't care about *me* at all, not the way I am now; she just wants Kathy back!'

Dr Perrin nodded slowly. 'Is that really the case, do you think?'

'Yes!'

'You don't think she cares about you?'

I fell into silence, glowering down at the pale beige carpet. 'Oh, I guess she does . . . She's just desperate for the old me to come back, and it's like who I am now doesn't count. I guess . . .' I trailed off, the words sticking in my throat.

'Yes?' asked Dr Perrin gently.

I wiped my eyes. 'I guess . . . that she and Kathy, she and the old me, must have been really close, or something. So now she wants her old daughter back.'

Dr Perrin was silent for a moment, gazing down at her notes. Finally she put them on her desk and said, 'You know, amnesia can be a frightening thing for families, Kat. Inevitably, there are questions asked – *Did we do this or that right? Was it our fault?* Perhaps your mother feels that if you got your memory back, she could feel reassured on some of these points.'

I stared at her, trying to translate all of this. 'You mean – she thinks it's her fault?'

Dr Perrin lifted a round shoulder. 'It wouldn't be uncommon.'

'But why would it be her fault?'

'Probably no reason at all. But fears aren't always logical, Kat.'

I could feel the black hole inside me, and I wondered whether my fear of Jade and the others been logical. Or had I known that something worse than being hit by a car would happen if I didn't run?

Dr Perrin smiled at me. For some reason it didn't seem as though she had as many teeth as usual. 'I'll see you on Wednesday for your regular appointment, Kat. Now, will you send your mother in to have a quick chat before you go?'

'She said it might mean something and it might not,' came Beth's muffled voice. I pressed against the stairwell, listening. The wallpaper felt smooth and cool against my ear.

'Is that all?' asked Richard. His voice sounded more serious than I had ever heard it.

'No . . . no, that's not all.'

Beth's voice broke, and a moment later I sat up straight as sobs floated up the stairs. I could hear Richard saying, 'That's right . . . just let it all out.' My pulse pounded as I listened. Beth was sobbing her eyes out like a little girl.

Her voice sounded strangled as she said, 'I'm sorry . . . I'm sorry. It's just – oh, Richard, she asked to see me privately, and she said she's almost certain now that the trauma that caused Kat's amnesia *wasn't* the car accident, that it was something else, something emotional . . .'

An icy bolt of fear shot through me. Had whatever happened at school been so bad that I had wiped out my whole memory? Oh my God, what had *happened* to me?

'She said – that maybe Kat was already so upset about something that her mind took the accident as an excuse to withdraw, or else it was just the last straw for her, in a way . . .' Beth's voice was so low I could hardly hear it.

'Any ideas?' said Richard.

'No! I've been trying to think, but there's nothing. We went through a lot with her father, but that was *years* ago. And I know she was angry with me over you moving in, but that was really just teenage stuff, nothing serious . . . I don't know what it could have been!'

'Do you think we should tell her?' asked Richard.

A honking sound, like Beth blowing her nose. 'No . . . no . . . we're to just let her regain her memory in her own time. If it ever comes back at all, that is.' She gave a shaky laugh. 'Doctor Perrin said that some amnesiacs *never* get back certain parts of their memories, that some things are lost forever. It depends on – on how traumatic the original experience was. Oh, Richard, *what* could have happened to her?'

I couldn't listen to any more. I crept back to my room and stood against the closed door, staring around me. Think! There had to be answers in this room somewhere, there *had* to be!

My gaze fell on Kathy's computer, and my heart jumped. Of course – there'd be emails, documents, all kinds of things! I leaped for the computer and turned it on, fumbling with the switch.

The screen lit up – a blue background with a long, narrow white box on it. A black line flashed inside the box, with PLEASE ENTER PASSWORD written above it. The cursor flashed at me, waiting. I frowned at the screen, and then slowly typed a word, looking down at the keys.

VIOLIN.

I hit 'Return'.

INVALID PASSWORD.

Cat, I typed.

INVALID PASSWORD.

Black clothes. Orlando. Pop music.

INVALID, INVALID, INVALID.

I tried every other word I could think of, but none of them were right. Finally I gave up and went to bed, turning out the light and wrapping the duvet tightly around myself. Why had I even bothered trying? Kathy was still a total stranger to me; I had no idea what her password might be.

I persuaded Beth to let me walk to school the next morning. She insisted on drawing a map for me, putting a big X where our house was, and another one at the school. 'Are you *sure* you know the way?' she kept asking.

I nodded, putting the map in my new coat pocket. 'I'll be fine.'

She didn't look at all convinced. 'Well, ring me if you get lost.' She stood at the door as I left, watching me with her arms folded over her chest. Richard appeared behind her, eating a piece of toast.

'We'll send a Saint Bernard after you if we don't hear from you soon,' he called, waving.

That made me laugh. 'Thanks,' I called back.

I had thought that if I walked to school like Kathy did, it might help me get into her head – but I hadn't expected the dizzying sense of *freedom* that soared through me once I left the house. It was the first time I had been alone, really alone, since I woke up after the accident.

I walked slowly, breathing in the crisp air, savouring the fact that I wasn't being stared at. No one paid any attention to me at all; cars whizzed past like I was just another student on her way to school. It was *brilliant.*

I passed a small park and paused, looking in at the empty slides and swings. On impulse, I creaked open the flaking-paint gate and went inside.

Sitting on one of the narrow red swings, I pushed myself gently back and forth, the chains squeaking in protest. My shoulder didn't hurt so much any more, I realized suddenly. I guessed the exercises were doing some good.

I wrapped my arms around the chains and leaned back, looking up at the gun-metal sky. Had my dad ever pushed me on a swing, back in Bournemouth?

My dad. I let out a breath, slowing down the swing.

What I hated most of all was that my memory-glitch, or whatever it had been, had interrupted the talk about my dad, and now I didn't know how to get it back again. I thought of the photo I had seen at Nana's, of him standing on the beach staring intensely at the camera.

He had looked so big, so solid. It was impossible to imagine him as a little boy, being abused. It was so awful, that that had happened! My hands gripped the chains. I wished I had asked Nana for that photo. I'd get it from her next time.

The thought hit me like a lightning bolt. I didn't have any photos of my dad. Not a single one.

I was almost late to school, and had to run the last little bit, my bag bumping against my legs. Poppy stood at the front gates waiting for me. I thought about running straight past her, but I didn't. I jogged to a stop.

'Hi,' she said stiffly.

I just looked at her, gripping the strap of my bag. The stone cat was nestled inside, and my spine straightened at the thought of him. She and Jade were *not* going to scare me. I'd find out what had happened whether they wanted me to or not.

Poppy glanced at her watch. 'Come on, we'd better go.'

When we got inside, Mrs Boucher was talking to the lady at the reception desk. She saw me and smiled, beckoning us over. She had short blonde hair like an elf, and wore a brown dress with a cardie over it. 'Kat! How are you doing? How was your first day yesterday? Your teachers all seem to think it went really well.'

'It was great,' I said, trying not to look at Poppy. 'I mean, I don't know how well I'm doing yet, but—'

Mrs Boucher waved this off. 'It'll take time; there's no hurry. Everyone's willing to help you as much as you need.'

Then she seemed to notice Poppy for the first time, and she frowned. 'Poppy? Where's Tina? Isn't she meant to be Kat's FAB buddy?'

'Oh, we all wanted to help Kat,' said Poppy. 'Jade, Tina and me. So we're taking turns. Is that OK, Miss?' Her cheeks reddened a bit, but she sounded completely natural. *Earnest*, even, like she was afraid Mrs Boucher might say no and then she would be really gutted.

Mrs Boucher just laughed, looking delighted that I was so popular even with no memory. 'It's fine with me, so long as Kat has the support she needs. Is it all right with you, Kat?'

I lifted my lips into something like a smile. 'Sure,' I said.

As Poppy was walking me to RE, Jade came up alongside us in the corridors and slammed into me, so that I stumbled and almost fell. I stared after her, swallowing hard. Tina caught up with her, and the two of them glanced back at me. Tina looked worried, but when she saw me watching her she tossed her head and hooked her arm through Jade's.

Poppy was still walking along like nothing had happened, staring straight ahead. I grabbed her arm. 'Look, you have to tell me what's going on!'

Her eyes flashed, and she shook me off. 'You *know* what's going on! What do you want, a written essay?'

'I *don't* know!' I cried. 'Can't you see that? Why do you all hate me so much? Did I do something? What?'

Poppy hesitated, biting her lip. We were standing in the middle of the corridor like rocks in a stream, with students sweeping round us on either side. For a moment I thought she was going to say something, but then her mouth hardened. 'We're going to be late,' she said.

Chapter Sixteen

Kathy

27 February

This morning I tried to pretend I was ill again. But Mum wanted to take me to the doctor, and I was afraid he'd tell her I was lying and then she'd find out what I did. So I had to go to school, and of course Jade came over to me first thing. She was angrier than I'd ever seen her. 'You took Tina's violin from outside the band room on Friday afternoon, didn't you?' she said.

I told her, NO, of course not! I could feel my face heating up, though. She just glared at me, and walked away.

Tina looked like she had been crying when I saw her. I wonder if she's told her dad? What if he rings Mum?! Not that anyone has any proof: no one saw me or anything. I'll just lie if he rings, and say I don't know what he's talking about. Anyone could have taken it.

I wish I could go back to Friday and just leave it there. I wish that *so much.*

Then later Jade passed me a note during RE. It

said: *Tina doesn't want to say anything because she's not positive it was you, but I am! Give it back or else!!!*

I wrote on it: *Or else what? I didn't take it!*

She read it with this steely glare on her face, and then mouthed 'tomorrow' at me when Mrs Randolph wasn't looking. I kept my face totally blank, like she wasn't getting to me at all, but in fact I'm scared. There's no way I can bring it to school tomorrow – Mum would see it! And I don't want anyone to know I took it anyway, I want to just dump it outside Tina's house or something!

In fact, that's what I planned to do when I got home this afternoon. I told Mum I was going for a walk, and then I planned to go to Tina's house (if I could even find it again) and leave it on their front doorstep.

But when I got out to the shed, I opened up the case and I just couldn't. It was so beautiful. I didn't dare play it, but I stroked one of its strings, very gently. It vibrated under my finger, so that I could feel the note humming through me. I kept thinking of Mrs Patton smiling at me and saying, 'Very good, Kathy, but a bit more vibrato in those final few bars.'

Anyway, I sat out there like a total numpty for ages, and then the next thing I knew it was getting dark and it was already way too late to try to go to Tina's. God, *why* did I even take it in the first place?!

I didn't mean to, I honestly didn't. I just saw it outside the band room, piled up with a bunch of other instruments – I think everyone was waiting for Mr Yately to come and open the door or something – and then the next thing I knew I had shoved it under my coat and I was walking away as quickly as I could, before anyone noticed. Then all the way home I was completely panicking, and thinking that I should throw it behind some bushes or something, but I couldn't just *abandon* it. What if it got damaged or something?

What am I going to do? What if Jade tells my mum?

Later

I was doing the dishes with Mum tonight, and part of me wanted to tell her everything – just let it all spill out, so that she'd tell me what to do and everything would be OK again. But she was upset about some client of hers who hasn't paid his bills, and Richard kept going in and out of the kitchen, saying things like, 'You're far too nice, love, you need to supply him with a two-week notice . . .' and so I just couldn't.

28 February

This morning Jade and Susan and Gemma started bumping against me in the corridors, really hard, hissing, '*Give it back, give it back.*' I told them I didn't have it, and Jade sneered at me and said, 'Oh, right!' Then they bumped against me so hard that I've got a bruise on my arm now.

Tina didn't join in, but I saw her watching, looking really upset. Poppy just stares at me, like she can't believe she was ever my friend. I made it through the day without crying, but only just. I will NOT let them see me cry, no matter what.

I need to take it back! But of course it was raining this afternoon, so I couldn't very well pretend to go for a walk. I did manage to slip out to the shed and make sure the violin was well covered up. Too much damp can ruin them.

Then I took it out of its case, just to make sure it was OK, and somehow I ended up playing it. I played a Mozart concerto – one of his early ones that he wrote when he was a child genius. I played really softly, so that Mum wouldn't hear, and at first I could hardly hold the bow right, I was so glad to be playing again. But it wasn't like I had thought.

It was awful. I kept waiting for the feeling of – of losing myself in the music, of drifting away and becoming part of it, but it didn't happen. Instead the music stayed totally separate from me, like a wall that I couldn't climb over, and it was so happy and light that it made me feel even heavier and darker, until when I finished I felt like . . .

Like. I don't know.

I hate myself.

Mum and Richard tried to talk to me during tea, but I didn't feel like saying very much. I must have been mad last night to think I could tell Mum. I can't tell anyone, ever.

1 March

Tina came up to me in the library today, and asked if I was the one who took her violin. I told her no, of course not, and she said, 'Look, I won't tell anyone if you did. But I need it back. It was my grandfather's, and my dad would be so upset if anything happened to it.'

I felt like crying then, but I just told her again that I didn't have it. And she bit her lip and said, 'Well, if you *did* have it – I mean, just supposing – then do you think maybe you could bring it back tomorrow? You could give it to me in the girls' loo, the one by the gym. No one would see you. Please?'

I wondered then if Jade and the others were going to be there, but Tina knew what I was thinking and said, 'Just us, I promise. I only want the violin back, that's all. Please, please, give it back!'

So I said OK. I couldn't look at her or anything. I felt so ashamed. She didn't say anything else, she just sort of nodded and walked off. I'll have to smuggle it to school in my bag or something tomorrow, without Mum seeing. Thank God, at least it will be over with then!!

Later

I just woke up from a nightmare. I'm shaking so bad I can't get back to sleep. It was awful, so totally awful. Richard was shouting at me, and his face started twisting and changing, turning red, and then it wasn't Richard at all, it was some sort of demon. Mum and I hid in a closet from him, all huddled together while he raged around, and she was crying because she had thought that Richard was nice, and he had turned out to be like this. And I couldn't say anything to her, because I knew it was all my fault he had changed.

I feel so scared. What if that's true? I mean, what if

Dad changed because of me? He and Mum must have been happy once – something had to happen to change things. And babies can do that; I read in this magazine that they can put a lot of strain on a marriage. Maybe Dad just couldn't deal with it.

I really don't want to believe that. I don't want for it all to have been my fault! But I can't think of anything else it could have been.

Chapter Seventeen

Kat

I sat alone in RE, not even pretending that I was with Poppy. The teacher, Mrs Randolph, was about eighty-two and didn't seem to notice that I was on my own. She droned away about Catholicism for ages, making it about ten times more boring than it probably had to be. I stared down at my exercise book, drawing pointless circles in the margins. The scar on my forehead itched, like an irritating insect was walking across my skin.

I looked up. Mrs Randolph had started passing out worksheets, her hands trembling arthritically. 'Get into groups, everyone. Take a few minutes to discuss, and then work through the answers together.'

Suddenly everyone was scraping their chairs together into exclusive little clusters. Naturally Jade, Tina and Poppy all sat together. None of them looked at me.

'Kat needs a group,' announced Mrs Randolph in her raspy voice, squinting at the class through her glasses. 'Who needs another person?'

Hardly anyone even glanced up; they were all too

busy buzzing away in their groups. I bit my lip, feeling like I had a sign pinned to my back: IGNORE THIS GIRL. SHE IS TO BE SHUNNED AT ALL COSTS!

'Kat, do you want to sit with us?' called a voice.

My chin jerked up as relief flooded through me. A girl with a thin face and long auburn hair was smiling at me, pointing to an empty seat beside her. Her friend had light blonde hair held back by a black hair-band. She was smiling at me too.

I didn't need a second invitation. I scooped up my bag and moved over to them, weaving my way round the tables. Pulling out a chair, I sat down between them. 'Hi,' I said shyly.

The blonde girl leaned forward. 'Do you really have amnesia?' she whispered.

I was getting incredibly sick of that question, but I couldn't very well refuse to answer it when they had just rescued me from being an outcast. I nodded. 'Yeah, I really do.'

They looked at each other. 'So . . . you don't remember us?' asked the auburn-haired girl. She had a pendant of a running horse around her neck.

I shook my head.

She blinked. 'That's so weird. Well . . . I'm Rachel and this is Holly.'

'Were you friends of mine? From before, I mean?' I hated how hopeful I sounded, like a plaintive three-year-old.

Holly shrugged. She had light blue-grey eyes and a snub nose. 'Sort of, I guess. You sat with us at lunch sometimes.'

I glanced over my shoulder at Mrs Randolph, but she practically looked asleep at her desk. I crossed my elbows on the table, leaning forward. 'Do you know why Jade and the others hate me? They won't tell me what's going on.'

Rachel made a face. 'Oh, don't worry about it. Jade and that lot are always falling out over something.'

'But – I mean, I sort of think it's more than that.'

She shrugged. 'Well, you can always sit with us; we don't mind.' She glanced at Holly. 'Hol, did I tell you about Champion this morning?'

Holly leaned forward. 'No, what?'

Rachel fingered her pendant, grinning. 'We jumped three foot six! He was so good, he didn't even hesitate. Mum says I can enter him in the next competition.'

Holly gasped, and gave a little bounce. 'That's great! We can enter together!'

'Oh, are you entering with Daisy?'

They kept on like that for the rest of the class, whispering about horses or ponies or whatever, and forgetting I was even there. I gazed down at the worksheet. There was a long paragraph about Catholicism, and then a bunch of questions. *What percentage of the world's population is of the Catholic faith?* I slowly wrote down the answer.

Was that all it was? Had I just *fallen out* with Jade and the rest of them? Maybe I had misunderstood everything. I looked over at Jade's table.

Jade shot me a gaze, her dark hair like a cape over her shoulders. Her eyes were slits.

* * *

'That's it!' cried Richard. 'Eight of clubs, that was my card. Well done! You've really been practising, haven't you?' He beamed at me.

I smiled, shuffling the cards against the dining table. 'Yeah, sort of.' Radio 3 played in the background – a ballet by someone called Prokofiev, with dramatic drums and trumpets.

Richard laughed. 'Sort of, nothing. Are you up for learning another one, to add to your repertoire?'

'Sure, go on.' It was better than worrying about Jade and the others, anyway. I hooked my leg under me, leaning forward on my elbows. Richard took the deck and cut it.

It was just the two of us; Beth was upstairs talking to one of her clients on the business phone. She hated making evening appointments, but said that sometimes people couldn't talk to her any other time.

'Right, now for this trick, you—'

'Wait,' I gasped, clutching his arm.

Richard stopped, his reddish eyebrows drawing together. 'Kat? What is it?'

'The music! Listen!' The ballet had ended, and now the most beautiful music I had ever heard was wrapping around us. A single violin, soaring like a bird against the low, gentle pulsing of an orchestra. It was like – heaven and earth, embracing each other.

Tears came to my eyes as the violin effortlessly dipped and flew, reaching up and up. I don't know how long we sat there and listened, but finally the music ended, and my fingers fell away from Richard's arm. 'I have to know what that was! Richard, we have to find out!'

He squeezed my hand and stood up. 'Not a problem. We'll just hop onto the BBC website and get the playlist.'

He picked up his briefcase from beside the sofa, and snapped it open on the dining table. Taking out his laptop, he plugged it into the downstairs phone line, and a few moments later we were looking at the Radio 3 website, scrolling down a list of entries.

'What's the time, just past seven?' Richard stroked the cursor pad and tapped at the black keys. 'Right . . . that was Bach's Concerto Number One in A minor, for Violin and Orchestra. The *andante* movement.'

'The *what*?' Peering over his shoulder, I stared at the words on the screen. How could such a boring title have anything to do with that incredible music?

'The slow movement. Concertos are divided into several parts, I think.' He reached for the cursor again.

'No, hang on, I have to write down what it's called!' I ran into the kitchen to grab a Post-it pad from the drawer where Beth kept pens and batteries and things, and then dashed back into the dining room. 'OK, what's it called again?'

Richard read it out to me, and I wrote it down carefully, drawing a line under it. 'There,' I said, peeling off the Post-it sticker. 'Now I just have to *find* it.'

Richard glanced at me and smiled. Closing down

the laptop, he said casually, 'You know, I think it's late-night shopping in town tonight, if you fancy popping along to the music shop.'

Beth was in the kitchen when we got back, scowling at the kettle as it boiled. Richard gave her a hug from behind, kissing her hair. 'How did it go? Was that Mrs Perlman again?'

Beth sighed as she made a cup of tea. '*Yes.* She never listens to a word I say; I don't know why she's even bothering to do life-coaching. Never mind . . .' Looking over at me, she smiled. 'Did you find what you were after?'

'Yes, look!' I took the CD out of the bag and showed it to her. 'It's Bach's Concerto Number One in A minor, for—'

'For Violin and Orchestra,' finished Beth softly. A strange expression crossed her face as she examined the CD. She looked at me, her fingers tightening on the plastic case. 'You just heard this tonight?'

I nodded, wondering what was wrong. She put the CD down on the worktop, angling it carefully so that it lined up with the edge. 'Did you – did you remember anything when you heard it?' Her voice sounded strained.

Not *that* again! I shoved the CD back in the yellow and red plastic bag. 'No. I just liked it, that's all.'

'Oh.' She gazed down at her tea.

'Beth, what is it?' asked Richard, touching her arm.

She swallowed, tried to smile as she glanced at me. 'It's just – Kat, that's the piece you used to love so much, the Bach violin concerto I told you about. You used to play it over and over again.'

It felt like she had just splashed a bucket of ice-water over me. 'I liked this before?'

Beth nodded. 'You loved it. So when I saw it, I just thought . . .' She trailed off and lifted a shoulder, grimacing. 'Sorry.'

I sat on the floor of my room, hugging my knees and listening to the music. It was just as beautiful as it had been on the radio, but somehow I couldn't relax enough to let it pick me up and carry me away. I kept thinking of how I used to play the violin.

Why had I stopped? Grade five, that sounded so impressive! Had I been as good as the violinist on the CD? I traced a pattern on the carpet, listening to the music. Probably not, I guessed, since I was only ten or something when I stopped playing – but it sounded like I *could* have been that good someday, if I had kept at it.

Was it what I had wanted to do with my life? Because in the photo where I had been standing up on stage, you could tell that I loved playing; that I really, really loved it. So why had I stopped even listening to classical music? You don't just stop liking something, do you?

No. You don't.

Suddenly my heart beat faster, and I stared at the computer. I had liked the same things when I was

Kathy as I did now, even if I had tried to stop, for some reason. The concerto proved it.

I jumped up and switched on the computer. The cursor blinked at me inside the white box. PLEASE ENTER PASSWORD.

I took a deep breath and typed: BACH.

A jangle of computer-music blared from the speakers as the blue screen disappeared, and a scene of a rolling green hill in front of a cloud-filled sky took its place. A line of brightly coloured icons marched down the left-hand side of the screen.

I was in. I slid into the chair, staring at the icons.

WORD. EMAIL. INTERNET. SOLITAIRE.

I tried WORD first, glancing through the old documents, but there wasn't much there – just some old school papers I had written. I clicked onto EMAIL and the screen changed again.

Now I was looking at a white background with rows and rows of email titles. I fumbled with the keys, scrolling down. There were *hundreds* of them! They went back years! And . . . my skin prickled.

Almost every single one of them was from Poppy or Jade.

Hours later, my skull was throbbing from squinting at the tiny print. I leaned back in the chair and rubbed my eyes. They felt rough and gritty.

I hadn't completely believed it before, but the three of us really had been fantastic mates – always going off to the cinema together, or going shopping, or doing homework together. Hardly a night had gone by without a couple of emails flying back and forth. But then they just *stopped*, about three weeks before the car hit me.

Just stopped. And now Poppy and Jade probably wouldn't spit on me if I were on fire.

I jumped as a knock rapped on my door, shattering the silence. The CD had ended ages ago. 'Yes?' I called, turning round in my seat.

Beth stuck her head round the door. 'Can I come in?'

My neck heated up, and I hastily clicked the screen away. 'Sure. I was just . . . looking at the computer.'

Her eyes widened as she hurried into the room, shutting the door behind her. '*Really?* Have you remembered the password, then?'

I shook my head, hating how excited she looked. 'No, I just guessed it. It took me ages.'

'Oh.' She let out a breath. Neither of us said anything for a moment, and then she gave me a small smile. 'I tried to get onto it while you were in hospital, but I couldn't work out the password.'

I stared at her. 'You tried to get onto it when I wasn't even here?'

'I was worried about you. Did you—?' She cleared her throat. 'I mean, is there anything there that – that might explain things?'

Things. You mean why I lost my memory? I shook my head, playing with the space key on the keyboard. 'No. Just a bunch of old emails, that's all.'

'Nothing that . . . has any unresolved questions around it?'

I would have smiled at that, if I hadn't been so irritated that she sounded like Dr Perrin. 'No. Just lots of emails to Poppy and Jade. About parties and stuff.'

Beth sighed. 'So long as I'm confessing, I tried to find your journal too.'

My throat went dry. 'I . . . kept a journal?'

'Yes, I've seen you writing in it. You must have kept it well hidden, though.' The corners of her mouth lifted faintly.

I stared around the small room, my mind racing. But I had looked absolutely everywhere! Where could I have hidden a journal?

Beth rubbed her elbow. 'Anyway, that's not why I came in. Kat, I just wondered if – if you'd like me to get you another violin.'

I looked up. 'What?'

'A violin,' she said softly. 'Like you had before.'

'But—' I stared at her. 'Don't I already have one, somewhere?'

Her cheeks reddened. 'No, it – got broken when we moved. I hired one for you for a while, but then you said you weren't interested any more, and I shouldn't bother. So I just wondered – I mean, now that we can afford it, and you seem to like classical music again – whether you'd like another one.'

I thought of the Bach concerto, and a chill of excitement flickered through me. I looked down, trying to hide it. 'But I don't know how to play.'

'No, not now.' She sat down on my bed. 'But if you

wanted to take lessons again, I bet you'd pick it up really quickly, because you were so advanced before. And it might help bring back your memory too.'

My head snapped up. She sat very still, looking hopeful. 'Oh, Kat, it's worth a try, isn't it?' she burst out. 'I mean, we've tried everything else.'

I might have known! Naturally this was all just about getting my memory back. That was all she cared about!

'No, thanks,' I said. I clicked onto *Solitaire* on the computer.

'But, Kat—'

'I don't want to play the violin.' Maybe I did, but I wasn't about to do it with Beth listening anxiously to every note I played. *Have you remembered yet? No? Well, how about now?*

'Look, maybe if I just got you one – you don't have to take lessons right away. You could just play it on your own and see—'

I slammed down the mouse. '*No!* I don't want to!'

'You're not even trying!' Beth burst out. 'Kat, we have to get your memory back, you can't just *stay* like this!'

'Why not?' I cried. 'What's so terrible about the way I am now?'

'Nothing's *terrible* about it, it's just not you! It's like—' She broke off, biting her lip.

'What?' I asked.

She shook her head quickly. 'Nothing.'

Anger flashed through me. Suddenly I hated her, really hated her. 'You mean it's like I'm not even your daughter any more, don't you? Like you don't even know me!'

Beth ducked her head down and wrapped her arms tightly around herself. 'You don't even call me Mum any more,' she whispered.

'Because I only met you a couple of weeks ago!' I shouted. 'You don't *feel* like my mum! Do you think you can just – just be my mum *automatically*?'

'But I *am* your mum! I – oh, Kathy . . .' She buried her head in her hands. It felt like she had kicked me in the stomach. I sat there, frozen, with hot tears that couldn't begin to thaw me clutching at my throat.

Finally Beth sniffed and stood up, brushing the creases from her trousers. Her nose was red. 'I'm sorry. You're right. Just – think about the violin, OK? I want you to be happy, Kat, that's all.' She gave me a shaky smile and left the room, closing the door gently behind her.

Chapter Eighteen

Kathy

2 March

I haven't gone to school yet. I slipped out to the shed first thing, before Mum or Richard was up, and now I've got the violin all packed in my bag. As well as I can pack it, anyway. It sort of sticks out, but I've draped a jumper over the top of it. Now I just need to slip out of the house without Mum seeing it. Fingers crossed.

Oh God, I just want to get this over with! Find Tina and give her her stupid violin back, and—

No, stop. I can't cry now, Mum will see me with my eyes all red and ask questions.

Anyway, this is it. And then when I get home today it'll all be over. Finally and completely.

Chapter Nineteen

Kat

Poppy was waiting for me at the front gates again. I grabbed her arm and dragged her over to one side. 'I've got to talk to you.'

'What?' Her eyes bulged. She glanced over her shoulder, no doubt looking for Jade and the rest of her posse to come and protect her.

I opened my bag and thrust a sheaf of papers at her. 'Here.'

'What—?' She glanced through them, her forehead creasing. 'These are just old emails.'

'Almost *two years'* worth, actually,' I snapped. 'I just read through them last night. It proves we were really friends, doesn't it?'

She stared at me. 'Kat, of course we were friends. But—'

'And look, see—' I rifled through the pages, pointing at a date. 'The emails just *stopped* here, only a few weeks before the car hit me. One minute you and Jade are talking about some party I missed, and then the next you're gone! So what happened?' My voice trembled. 'You were both my friends, and then you just dumped me? Or what?'

Poppy stood there holding the emails, looking dazed. I saw her throat move as she swallowed. A laughing group of sixth-formers walked past, and she edged out of their way, not taking her eyes off me.

'You . . . really don't remember, do you?' she said slowly.

I should have felt elated, but instead I just wanted to smack her one. 'Oh, whatever gave you *that* idea? You mean you only just now realized?' I grabbed the emails back from her, stuffing them into my bag. A tear crept down my face, and I swiped it away.

Poppy started to say something and then stopped, looking over her shoulder again. She nibbled on the side of her thumb. 'Kat, um . . . why don't we go to the park?'

The sound of students drifting into the school seemed to fade around us. I stared at her. 'You mean not go to school?'

Poppy nodded. 'Just for the first lesson, then we can sneak back. It's Mrs Randolph again, she probably won't even notice.' She flushed. 'I – I've got a lot to tell you.'

We sat side by side on the swings, pushing them gently with our feet and letting our legs drift from side to side. Poppy glanced at me, looking nervous. 'Um . . . I like your coat. It's pretty, that shade of red.'

I let out a breath. 'Look, just tell me, OK? Whatever it is.'

So she did. All of it – how I had hated Richard

moving in, how I had liked Tina at first but then seemed to turn against her. And how I had stolen Tina's violin.

My heart jumped off a cliff. 'I *what*?'

Poppy licked her lips. 'From outside the band room. A bunch of people had left their instruments piled up there, because they were waiting for Mr Yately to come and open the door. And while they were all at the window, watching the football team practise . . . I guess you just stole it.'

'Maybe it wasn't me! I mean, did anyone see me? Or – or did I say anything about it?' My words spilled out on top of each other.

Poppy sighed. 'It was you. You admitted it to Tina. And you told her that you'd give it back to her, but—' She stopped.

'What?' I whispered. My heart was beating so loudly I could hardly hear her.

She bit her thumb. 'I don't know. Something happened, but I don't know what. Tina told Jade, but she made her swear not to tell anyone else. She's . . . really, really upset over whatever it was. So's Jade. She's been trying to get Tina to go to Mrs Boucher, but she won't do it.'

I swallowed hard. What had I done? God, what had I done?

Poppy looked quickly up at me, her eyes bright with tears. 'Kat, I'm sorry for not believing you, I really am! But it just seemed so – I mean, Jade said you did something *terrible* to Tina, and then the very next day you got bumped by a car and said you had amnesia . . .' Her voice faded off to nothing.

'That's OK,' I said. My voice felt like sandpaper scratching at my throat. 'I understand.'

Jade didn't come near me at lunch, or in the corridors. I was desperate to talk to Tina, to apologize and try to find out what had happened, but Jade stuck to her side like superglue.

PE was the last class of the day. The teacher, Mrs Waites, had us climbing these ropes hanging from the ceiling, pulling ourselves up them like monkeys gone wrong. 'Grip with your knees!' she kept shouting.

When we went into the changing rooms after the class ended, my bag was gone.

'Where did you leave it?' asked Poppy.

'Here! Right here, on this bench!'

'Are you sure?' She peered under the bench, like maybe it was hiding there.

'Yes! I'm completely sure; it's just not here any more!' I was close to tears. The cat statue was in my bag! *Kathy's* statue. Mine.

I looked across the changing rooms to where Tina and Jade stood talking. Jade's expression was intense. Tina just looked scared. She shook her head and then she glanced over and saw me watching. Her cheeks flooded with colour as her eyes hardened, and she nodded at Jade.

I gazed stupidly at her, thinking that her red face clashed with her ginger plaits. 'Do you think they have it?' I whispered to Poppy.

She stood staring at Tina and Jade. 'I don't know.

It definitely looks like they're up to something.'

My heart felt like it was doing a drum solo in my chest. 'Can't you find out? Can't you ask Jade after school and let me know?'

Poppy bit her lip. 'I can try, but I don't think she'll tell me. I tried to talk to her during science when you were at your other class, and . . . well, she's pretty narked that I believe you now.'

'Oh.' I swallowed hard and finished getting dressed, buttoning my shirt with cold hands. I glanced over at Tina and Jade again, and took a deep breath. 'Well . . . if they're up to something, then I guess I'll find out about it, won't I?'

'How have you been doing?' asked Dr Perrin, beaming at me. 'Any changes since last week?' Pen poised, at the ready.

I sat on the sagging green sofa, pulling the sleeve of my jumper over my hand. Changes. God, where did I even begin?

'Has something happened?' prompted Dr Perrin. Her hair was brighter than it had been last week, like it was freshly dyed, and it puffed out around her face, hair-sprayed to within an inch of its life as usual. But her eyes looked friendly. She smiled at me, waiting.

I looked up, licking my lips. 'Yeah, sort of.' I hesitated, glancing at her notebook, and blurted out, 'Could you put your pen down, maybe? And just listen?'

I couldn't *believe* I had said that. Dr Perrin looked

a bit taken aback, and then she quietly put her pen and notebook on her desk. She leaned forward, crossing her arms on her knees. 'Go on, Kat. What's going on?'

I told her everything, right from the start. When I finally finished, my cheeks were damp with tears. I had started crying about halfway through, and hadn't been able to stop, choking the rest of the story out between sobs.

Dr Perrin passed me a box of pale blue tissues without saying anything. I wiped my face, sniffing. I wondered how often her patients burst into tears. Maybe she had dozens of spare tissue boxes stashed away under her desk.

'What do you think I did to Tina?' I asked her. 'It must have been really awful.'

She frowned thoughtfully. 'Kat, I don't think that's quite the issue. Yes, of course you need to find out and make amends to this girl, but you also need to make amends to yourself. It sounds as though you were under a great deal of stress.'

I stared at her, clenching the soggy tissue in my hand. 'What do you mean?'

'Well, we don't know yet. But it sounds as though there were probably a lot of issues that had been building up inside you, bothering you for a very long time.'

I looked down, shredding a corner of the tissue. 'Like . . . like what?'

'It's hard to say. Maybe to do with your father, for instance.'

'My father?' My stomach dipped. I had hardly even

mentioned him. It was like she was reading my mind again, like she had done with my phoney dream!

Dr Perrin nodded. 'It's a possibility. I know from your history that your father died quite suddenly, after you and your mother left the family home. It would be surprising if there weren't unresolved issues there.'

I crumpled up the tissue and threw it at the bin. I missed. 'But that doesn't, like – give me an excuse to beat up Tina, or whatever it was I did!'

'Of course it doesn't,' she said gently. 'But people don't always behave in reasonable ways when they're in pain, and you have to make allowances for that. It's a matter of *understanding*, not excusing.'

I rubbed my fingers together, taking this in. I sort of got what she meant, but it still sounded like making excuses to me.

She went on. 'Given your amnesia, I think it's likely that something has been bothering you for a long time, something that has nothing to do with Tina at all. Perhaps she was the catalyst, but I doubt she was the cause.'

I looked up, the breath clenched in my throat. 'What do you mean?'

Dr Perrin smiled sadly at me. 'That's what amnesia is all about, Kat. The mind has a way of burying what it finds too painful to deal with. These things just fall away into the cracks, until the person feels strong enough to handle it.'

I sat on my bed listening to the Bach violin concerto, willing it to take away the events of the day. But they kept whirling about in my head, until I wanted to crawl away under the duvet and never come out again. How could I have done all that to Tina? How could I have *stolen her violin*? No wonder she hated me. I'd hate me too.

And now she and Jade had my cat statue. I swallowed. I wasn't totally sure why it meant so much to me, but it did. What if they didn't give it back to me? What if I never saw it again?

I picked up Barney the panda, stroking his matted fur. He stared at me with his single yellow eye. It looked worried. 'I don't blame you,' I muttered. I sat back against the wall, hugging him to my chest. He felt weirdly comforting for some reason.

The orchestra pulsed slowly, steadily, as the violin dipped and soared above it. I let out a breath as the music came to an end, wanting it to linger on in my mind. Instead I just saw Tina again, her cheeks reddening in the changing rooms as she glared at me.

Was Dr Perrin right? Was all this about Tina? Or something else? Suddenly I sat up straight, staring at my desk. *These things just fall away into the cracks* . . .

My pulse pounding, I threw Barney aside and scrambled off the bed. A moment later I was crouched on the floor, yanking all of the drawers out of the desk. The bottom one stuck a bit and I jostled it, wrestling it out of the unit.

Underneath where it had been there was a space about fifteen centimetres tall, hidden by the wooden front of the desk. It was the perfect hiding place.

Lying on the carpet was the CD that had dropped down . . . and a book.

I reached for it in slow motion. It had a shiny black cover with multi-coloured flowers on it. I touched one of the flowers, feeling the smoothness of the cover. The book felt heavy in my hands.

My ribs tightened in my chest. Part of me didn't want to open it. Part of me really, really didn't want to know what it said.

But I had to.

Sitting with my back to the desk, I opened my journal and began to read.

Chapter Twenty

Kathy

2 March
Later
Oh God.

I feel so ill, so horrible. I just keep seeing her face, over and over in my mind. And my face, in the mirror. I looked . . . No. I can't think about it.

When I got home from school today I was actually sick. Mum said something to me, and I just threw up, all over the floor. I couldn't stop retching. I think I threw up everything I've ever eaten. Then I came to bed, crawling under the duvet, just wanting to hide forever. Mum thinks I have food poisoning or something, because I'm shaking, and cold and hot at the same time. She can't find our thermometer, so she's gone to see if a neighbour has one she can borrow.

She just came back and took my temperature. I don't have a fever, apparently. 'Are you OK, angel?' she asked. She hasn't called me angel in years.

I shook my head, crying. Can't stop crying. She looked so worried. She'd hate me if she knew. Everyone would hate me. Everyone who doesn't already.

Later

Mum just came in again. She brought my dinner on a tray. There was a pink rose in a bud vase that she said Richard had brought home for me when she told him I wasn't well.

Why are they being so nice to me? Why?

I keep expecting someone to ring. Tina's dad, or the police or something. Nobody has. I'm so scared they will, but at the same time I don't think I'd even care.

I feel so ill. I hate myself so much.

The look on Tina's face . . . I don't even remember exactly what happened. I just know she said something like, 'Oh, thank God! I thought I'd never see it again!' Then she said, 'Just in time too. Dad's been wondering why I haven't played any duets with him lately.'

I hadn't given it back to her at that point, I had only just taken it out of my bag. And when she said that – I just froze. My hands felt clammy, and suddenly I thought my head might explode. And . . . that's when I did it.

I took her violin out of its case and smashed it against the sinks. I kept smashing it until the casing cracked, and then I threw it on the floor and stomped on it, again and again. And then I ran out. I don't even know how I got home – I can hardly remember it.

I've got Cat out from his hiding place and I'm holding him now, but he isn't helping. I keep thinking of that night. Over and over, the horrible noise it made. In fact, sometimes I think that Cat doesn't prove anything at all. Dad couldn't have loved me and did what he did. He couldn't have.

I'm so stupid. I shouldn't have written all this down. I hate it that it's in naked black and white forever, where anyone can read it. I just want to wipe it all from my mind, forget it ever happened.

Never mind. It doesn't matter anyway, because I'm going to get rid of this journal. I've just decided. I'll throw it away or burn it or something, and get a new one. I can hardly wait.

Fresh, empty pages, with nothing written on them.

Chapter Twenty-one

Kat

When Beth came up to tell me that tea was ready, I was still sitting by the desk, with the journal on the floor beside me.

'Kat?' She quickly closed the door behind her and crouched beside me, brushing my hair back from my forehead. 'Kat, what's wrong?'

I looked at her, and couldn't stop the tears coming. I shook my head, leaning against her, and she put her arms around me, holding me tightly.

'Darling, what *is* it? What's wrong?'

I struggled to talk. The words felt soggy in my throat. 'Mum . . . Mum, I've done something awful,' I whispered.

And I handed her the journal.

A long time later the three of us sat on the bed in Mum and Richard's room, with the journal lying beside us. Mum wiped her eyes. 'You were going through all that, and I didn't even know! Oh, Kat, I don't see how I can forgive myself.'

'Beth, you didn't know,' said Richard, touching her hand.

'That's the point! I should have done!'

I leaned against the headboard, hugging my knees to my chest. 'What . . . what happened the night we left? What did my father do?' The question felt cold, dangerous. Like dipping my hand into a box of snakes. But I had to know.

Richard glanced at Beth. 'Should I leave?' he asked softly.

'No!' I told him. 'No. I want you here.' I looked at Beth again. No . . . not Beth. Mum. It felt right now, calling her that.

'What happened?' I repeated.

She rubbed her hand across her eyes. They looked red and raw. 'The – the doctors said to let you remember everything on your own, but – oh, Kat, I'm just going to tell you. You deserve to know.'

I waited, watching her. She looked down, playing with a corner of the duvet. 'It . . . it was a very unpleasant scene. Well, to put it mildly.' She swallowed hard, glanced at me.

'Kat, your father could be violent,' she said softly. 'He used to hit me sometimes. I don't think he ever hit you, or hurt you physically, but . . . in a way, he did something worse.'

I felt like I'd shatter into a million pieces if I moved. Richard reached over and squeezed my hand. His eyes stayed on Beth's face, warm and gentle, but with an undercurrent of helpless anger I had never seen before.

Mum took a ragged breath. 'He – he didn't know we were planning to leave. I had to – get my courage up for a long time to do it, and then do it quickly, without him knowing, so he wouldn't be able to stop us.'

She looked down at her hands. 'We did it when I thought he was going to be out one afternoon; he was meant to be playing golf. But there was some sort of problem with his booking, and he came home early. In a foul mood already . . . which wasn't improved by catching us with our bags packed, loading up my car.'

Mum gave a funny little laugh. 'I was so scared, but I tried to stand up to him. I told him we were leaving, that the marriage was over . . . and he was calm about it. That scared me worse than anything else, that he was so calm. He let us keep loading up the car, and then, just when we were about to leave, I – I thought we should say goodbye to him, because I didn't know when you'd see him again. And he *could* be good to you, he really could . . . So we went back inside, and I saw that . . .' She stopped, closing her eyes.

'Stop,' I said shakily. Images were swarming into my mind, bursting out of the black hole like they wanted to devour me. 'I – I remember.'

It had taken ages for Mum and me to drag all our things out to the car. Usually Dad was the one who packed everything in the boot, arranging it so picture-perfectly that it all fit together like puzzle pieces, but now Mum was just sort of flinging stuff in as fast as she could.

She kept glancing back at the house with wide

eyes, her lips tight. I remember that so clearly. And I wanted to help her, just so that things would go faster and whatever explosion might come from Dad wouldn't come after all, but I didn't know what to do. So I just stood there in the street with my arms folded over my stomach. I didn't say anything, or ask her anything about where we were going. I thought I might be ill if I tried to talk.

Finally, finally, all our bags were in the car. Mum turned to look at me. 'Is that everything?' she asked.

And I nodded, because I thought it was. I hadn't realized yet.

Mum looked up at the house. 'Well – I guess we should go say goodbye,' she said. She sounded doubtful, like maybe she was hoping I'd say, 'No, actually, we really shouldn't, let's just go.'

But I didn't. Suddenly I was remembering all the good stuff about Dad. I looked up at the house and I wasn't sure about leaving any more. Maybe all dads were like this, maybe it was just how it was supposed to be. And it wasn't *that* bad, really, was it?

'Come on,' said Mum, holding her hand out to me. 'It won't take long, and then we'll go. It'll be OK.'

She looked like she hoped she was right.

So we went back into the house. And peeked into the lounge. And Dad's chair was empty. The TV was still on, but he was gone.

We both just stood there, staring. I don't know why it seemed like such a shock – so ominous, even. But it did. It felt very, very bad, in fact, and I was just about to say, *Let's forget about saying goodbye, let's just go,* when Dad appeared in the corridor leading from the bedrooms.

'You forgot this,' he said. He was holding up my violin case.

Mum went pale. 'You said you packed everything!' she hissed at me.

I couldn't move, couldn't speak. Because I *had* packed my violin. I would never have forgotten it, never in a million years. Dad must have found my packed bags the night before. He must have known all along what Mum was planning.

'Well, don't get any bright ideas about taking it,' said Dad. He pulled it out of its case and strummed a few chords, plucking his fingers over the strings. 'Because I paid for it, didn't I? Like I paid for everything else. Well, take the rest of it, go on. But you're not taking this.'

Mum glanced at me. You could see she was so terrified that I was going to make a scene, that I was going to start sobbing that I *had* to have my violin.

'Kathy, I'll get you another one,' she whispered. 'It's OK, I promise.'

I nodded. Staring at my violin in Dad's hand. He swung it about lazily, like he was pretending to play tennis. The tears felt hot and prickly against my eyes, but I wasn't going to cry. Wasn't going to give him the satisfaction.

He looked right at me and smiled. 'Going to say goodbye to your dad, Kathy?'

'Goodbye,' I whispered. It was my violin I was saying goodbye to, not him. I stared at it in his hand, swinging back and forth. What would he do with it? Would he sell it? Throw it away?

'*Goodbye,*' he mimicked. 'Is that it? The big goodbye scene? Come on, love – haven't you got a kiss for your old man?'

I hesitated, glancing at Mum. I was afraid that he'd try to grab me or something if I went near him, and I could see from Mum's face that she was scared of the same thing. 'No, we have to go now,' she told him loudly. 'We'll sort out visitation, and . . . all that later. OK?'

I knew that she meant to sound all bold and emancipated, but that final *OK?* showed her speech up for what it was – a plea for him to let us go. He wasn't holding us, he wasn't even touching us. God, he was standing about six metres away! But somehow we still needed his permission to leave. We were like helpless statues without it.

Suddenly Dad's face twisted. He pointed the violin at us like a curse, and I flinched. 'Fine then, just get out!' he shouted. 'Leave!'

'Hurry, Kathy, come on,' said Mum. She pulled at my arm, and I stumbled after her, still staring at my violin.

'Wait, Kathy! Wait a minute.'

His voice sounded so pleading suddenly that I turned back despite myself. Mum froze in the doorway, watching me. And then it happened.

Dad swung his arm back and smashed my violin against the wall.

I flinched so hard that it was like my skin tried to

jump off. I couldn't look away, couldn't move. Staring straight at Mum, he kept swinging his arm, bringing the violin down again and again, until the casing started to splinter. Then he threw my violin on the floor and stomped on it with his big foot. The strings twanged as it broke.

Giving Mum a final glare, Dad kicked the violin at her. It skidded across the floor, banging into the settee. 'Fine,' he said. 'So go. Good riddance.'

As we drove away, Mum wiped her eyes and said, 'Kathy, don't worry, love. I'll buy you another one. OK? It'll all be all right, I promise.'

'OK,' I said.

But I knew I never wanted to see another violin again.

Richard made hot chocolate with whipped cream for us, and we sat cross-legged on the bed drinking it. It helped, somehow. Not much, but a little. Maybe chocolate always does. I sipped mine slowly, savouring the rich sweetness.

Now that that bit of my memory had come back, I wished it would go away again; crawl back into the hole it had come from. Nothing else had come back yet, just that one snippet. The worst one; it had to be.

But there was still something I had to know. Glancing at the journal, I cleared my throat and said, 'Why . . . why didn't you let me go back to see Dad again? Before he died?'

Mum sighed. 'Because he didn't know where we were, and I didn't want him to find out. We were officially supposed to be dealing with each other only through lawyers, but he had got our new phone number somehow, and was being very unpleasant – ringing up, harassing me. He said he was going to take you away from me, and never let me see you again. And I believed him. Or at least I believed that he'd try if he could. I couldn't take the chance, Kat, I just couldn't.'

'You should have told me,' I whispered. Another bit of memory was floating back. Not a complete one, just remembering how *angry* I had felt, how frustrated that she wouldn't let me see him. Because despite everything I had wanted to, so badly! I knew that he'd be sorry, that he'd want to apologize for what he'd done. And – I needed him to. I needed that a lot.

'You're right,' said Mum. She took a ragged breath. 'I guess I was trying to shield you, but – but you're right. And then he had the heart attack before the divorce became final, and—'

'It was too late,' I finished. The lump in my throat felt like a rock.

Mum nodded. 'It was too late,' she echoed. 'And you had to live with the fact that the last time you saw him, he did that awful thing to you.'

She stirred her cream slowly, watching it dissolve. 'I guess I always knew that that was why you stopped playing,' she said softly. 'But I didn't want it to be the reason. It was such an awful thing to have happened, and I felt that I had bungled things so badly . . . After we moved here you had a new school and new friends, and you didn't *seem* bothered by it. That sounds so ridiculous now, but . . . but at the time it was easy to pretend that maybe you had just lost interest.'

'Stop blaming yourself,' said Richard, pressing her hand.

'Oh, I do,' said Mum grimly. 'But the important thing now is *you*, Kat. How are you feeling?'

Battered. Confused. Like a train has just run over me. I lifted my shoulder. 'I don't know.'

Richard cleared his throat and said, 'Kat, I don't think it was directed at you, daft as that sounds. I think it was Beth who your dad was really trying to get at – it was a power-play, a control thing . . . I'm sure he loved you very much.'

I nodded stiffly, trying to hold back the tears. 'I just . . . I can't believe that I did the same thing to Tina,' I whispered. 'Mum, how could I have done that?'

She put her arm around me, hugging me close. 'Kat, it's all right. I'll ring her father, and we'll make things right, somehow. We will.'

I took a deep breath. 'No. I've got to do it myself. I did it to her, and I've got to make it up to her.'

Mum shook her head. 'Kat, darling, you can't do it on your own. You need help.'

'But you didn't do it!' I cried. The hot chocolate, cold now, sloshed in its cup as I put it back on the tray. 'It was me! I can't hide behind you, I've got to make things right on my own!'

Mum and Richard looked at each other. Mum started to say something, and stopped.

'Let me try,' I pleaded. 'Let me just try, OK?'

'All right,' said Mum finally. 'But *talk* to me, Kat, OK? Let me know what's happening. And I'm going to have to ring her dad tomorrow after school, regardless.'

'OK,' I agreed softly. Guilt speared through me. Because I hadn't told her anything at all about what was happening at school, and I knew I wasn't going to.

It was for me to deal with, no matter how scared I was.

It was almost midnight when my mobile beeped with a new text: 2MORROW BEFORE SCHOOL, IN THE GIRLS' LOO BY THE CANTEEN. WE WANT 2 TALK 2 U.

Poppy was waiting for me inside the courtyard when I got to school the next morning. I showed her the text from Jade and she grimaced. 'Not good. She and Tina are definitely up to something.'

No, really? But that wasn't the important thing now. Tina was.

I put my mobile back in my coat pocket, and my fingers brushed against the deck of cards. For a second I couldn't think what they were doing there, and then I remembered sticking them in my pocket the day before, in case I had to wait ages to see Dr Perrin.

Great. I could impress Tina with card tricks; that would make up for everything.

I glanced at Poppy, tried to smile. 'I better go.'

'Do you want me to come with you?' Worry creased her round face.

I was holding a plastic carrier bag, and I shook my

head, tightening my grip on it. 'No. I'll tell you what happened later.'

'Kat! Are you *sure*? I could help, maybe, if—'

'No!' I snapped, gripping the bag so tightly that my fingers hurt. I took a deep breath. 'Sorry. No, OK? I've got to go.'

When I got to the girls' loo, Tina and Jade were there waiting for me. Jade leaned against the sinks with her arms over her chest. My bag was beside her, stuffed into the next sink along. Tina stood by the window, hugging herself.

Jade straightened up slowly when she saw me. 'I didn't think you'd come.'

I looked over at Tina. 'I had to. I – Tina, listen, I'm so sorry! I know what I did, and – and I don't know how I could have done it. I'm really, really sorry.'

Tina's cheeks reddened. 'Oh. Do you remember now?'

I flushed. 'No, not really – I—'

'No, you just wanted to get this,' interrupted Jade. She reached into my bag and took out the cat statue. She passed it from hand to hand, watching me.

'That's not why,' I told her. But my skin chilled, and I couldn't take my eyes off the cat. I saw my dad, swinging my violin back and forth. And suddenly another memory came into focus.

Cat. Dad had given me Cat, from his collection of ancient Egypt stuff. It was a real relic, thousands of years old, and had cost loads of money – but Dad knew how much I loved it, and he had just given it to me one day, without my even asking. I knew then that he had to love me. He really did, no matter how he acted sometimes.

'You took my bag,' I said to Jade.

She lifted a black eyebrow, giving me a level look. 'I didn't, actually.'

'No, *I* did.' Tina's chin jerked up.

'Why?' I whispered.

'Because it's what you did to me, isn't it?' Tina's voice trembled. 'It's only fair. Go on, Jade.'

'Right, then.' Jade held Cat up in the air, dangling him by the head. 'What we have here seems to be something that Kathy cares about, since she had it wrapped up so carefully in her bag. No, hang on – is it even yours?' she shot at me. 'Or did you steal *that* too?'

'It's mine,' I whispered. I stared at Cat, hanging so casually from her fingers above the hard tile floor. I wanted to talk to Tina, to tell her again how sorry I was, but the words froze in my throat.

Jade nodded. 'So you know what it's like to be *worried* about it, yeah?' She held Cat as high as she could over her head . . . and then let him drop. I gasped as she snatched him out of the air with her other hand.

Oh, please, I thought. Not Cat. It's the only thing I have from my dad . . .

Jade laughed. 'Not so nice, is it? Let's see, what shall we do next?'

'No! Tina, wait . . . I found this.' I scrambled to reach into the carrier bag, and pulled out my journal. Its shiny black cover glinted in the light.

'It's something I want you to read,' I said.

Frowning, Tina took the journal from me slowly, looking down at it. I swallowed, trying to find the right words. 'I think . . . I think I really liked you, Tina. But, Jade, you were right, I was jealous.' I glanced at her, still leaning against the sinks. Her dark eyebrows were drawn together uncertainly. 'I was jealous, and I couldn't deal with it. But I was completely wrong . . . and I'm sorry.'

Tina didn't move. She stood staring down at my journal, like she was trying to hold in a thousand emotions.

'Yeah, well maybe that's not good enough,' said Jade. 'You say you're sorry and that's it? Here you go, Tina, your choice.'

She tossed Cat to Tina. Tina looked up and caught him, fumbling a bit. I stiffened.

Tina stared at me, her eyes wide and uncertain. Then she dropped my journal onto the floor. It fell with a clatter, lying splayed and useless on the tiles. She held Cat up in the air, her hand deathly steady as her eyes bored into mine. 'Right, Kathy. This is what you deserve, isn't it?'

I felt hot and cold at the same time. 'Go on, then,' I said softly. 'Smash it.'

Her expression loosened with surprise. 'You can't care that much about it, then!'

'You're wrong,' I told her. My voice shook, and I swallowed hard. 'You're so completely wrong. It's – it's the only thing I have from my dad. But—' I glanced at

Jade. She stood frozen, staring at me. I looked back at Tina, and steeled my spine.

'Smash it,' I said.

She didn't move.

'Smash it!' I yelled. 'You know you want to do it, so go ahead!'

'Fine!' she screamed back. In a single motion she stretched her arm back and threw Cat against the wall.

'No!'

For a second I thought it was me who had shouted the word. But it was Jade. She lunged for the wall, grabbing Cat before he hit it.

I gasped, managing not to cry. Tina pressed a hand over her eyes. Her shoulders shook.

'Here.' Jade thrust Cat at me, her face contorted. 'Take it! We weren't going to actually *do* it.' She whirled round to face Tina. 'You weren't supposed to actually *do* it! We were just going to scare her, remember?'

Crying, Tina pushed past Jade and ran out of the door, just as the first bell rang.

I stared at Jade. 'Thank you,' I whispered, clutching Cat.

She turned quickly away, looking like she was going to burst into tears. 'Forget it! Just – forget it.'

I started to say something else and stopped. There'd be time to talk to Jade later. Shoving Cat in my pocket, I grabbed my journal and went after Tina, running as fast as I could.

Tina darted through the corridors, her ginger plaits flying. I pounded after her, weaving my way through the stream of black uniforms. 'Oi, watch where you're going!' snapped someone.

She ran straight out of the front door. I followed her, ignoring the receptionist, who stood up and called, 'You two girls! Get back here, you don't have permission to leave!' Her voice faded behind me as I ran down the front steps.

Once we were away from the school, Tina slowed to a brisk walk, hugging herself. I slowed down too, and she stopped suddenly, glaring over her shoulder at me. 'What do you *want*? Can't you just leave me alone?'

My footsteps echoed against the pavement as I came up alongside her. 'I'll leave you alone if you want,' I said softly. 'But I really want you to have this.' I offered her the journal again. 'Please? You don't even have to *read* it; you can burn it if you want! But please take it.'

She hesitated for a long moment. Finally she took it from me, holding it against her chest. Tears welled up in her eyes. 'You . . . you really had amnesia, didn't you?' she whispered. 'You weren't putting it on.'

I nodded, suddenly feeling totally exhausted. Like I could curl up on the pavement and sleep for a week. 'Yeah, I really had it. I still do, pretty much. I've remembered a couple of things, but . . .' I trailed off, not wanting to think about my dad. I'd have to at some point; I knew that, but . . . not now.

I gripped my elbow against my side. 'Why didn't you tell your dad what I did?' I asked. 'Or Mrs Boucher, or *somebody*?'

Tina's face crumpled a bit. She looked down at my

journal. 'I – I didn't want my dad to know. It was his father's violin; he'd be so upset – I mean, you can't imagine. So I just told him it was stolen, and *that* was awful enough.'

I took a trembling breath. 'Tina, look . . . I told my mum what I did. She's going to ring your dad tonight and talk to him about it . . . so he's going to find out what happened. I'm sorry. I'll tell her not to if you want, but – but I think she'll probably do it anyway.'

She bit her lip and didn't say anything for a moment. 'That's OK,' she said finally. 'I think he figured something was wrong anyway.'

Her fingers tightened on the journal. 'Kat . . . why did you run out into the road?'

'I don't know,' I said softly. 'I don't even know why I went to school that day, except – except I guess I was too ashamed to tell my mum what had happened. Maybe that's why I ran. I was too ashamed to face you; I wasn't even thinking straight.'

There was a long pause. Tina glanced over her shoulder at the school, and then at me.

'Do you want to bunk off?' she said.

It was probably the very last thing I had expected her to say. I gaped at her. 'What – together?'

Her eyes were a very clear blue, like chips of sky. She shrugged. 'Well, I don't really feel like going to school today. Do you?'

'No, but – what if someone catches us? The police or someone?'

She smiled. 'So what? I've always wanted a criminal record.'

* * *

We walked the mile or so into town, not talking much. And we didn't do all that much when we got there – we just bought a couple of sausage rolls and looked around the shops, trying a few things on. I glanced at my reflection, seeing a girl with wavy dark hair and green eyes who wasn't a stranger any more.

'There's nothing good here,' said Tina, putting a black miniskirt back on the rail. 'Let's go somewhere else.'

We wandered the rest of the way through town, and finally passed by a music shop, over by the library. Tina hesitated in front of the window, glancing at me. 'Do you want to go in?'

I nodded slowly, looking at the gleaming curve of saxophones on display. 'Sure.'

The violins were at the back. We stood looking at them without saying anything, but I knew that Tina felt the same as I did, that she was admiring how the light stroked the rich wood. A man with a black moustache came over to us, looking a bit suspiciously at our uniforms.

'Do you girls play?' he asked.

Tina nodded at the same time that I shook my head. She gave me an *oh, right!* look.

'You *do* play,' she said. 'You're miles better than me.'

My cheeks heated up. 'No, that was before! I don't know how any more.'

The man took one of the violins down. 'Has it been a while, then? Never mind, it soon comes back. Here, why don't you give it a go?'

I took the violin from him, even though I didn't have a clue how to hold it. It was heavier than I had expected. Tina helped me, arranging my fingers on the bow. 'There you go,' she said.

Feeling like an idiot, I stood up straight and pulled the bow across the strings. A sound like a screeching cat rang through the shop. I looked at Tina and we burst out laughing. 'OK, you were right,' she said. 'Bad idea.'

'Thanks anyway,' I said to the man, handing the violin back. He sniffed and adjusted it back on its stand very precisely, like he thought we had completely insulted it.

We bought sandwiches and crisps for lunch, and sat eating them on benches beside a small park. Tina drew her knees up to her chest and stared at the sky. 'This is nice,' she said.

'Yeah.' I gazed up at the clouds, remembering what Nana had said about seeing the world freshly. If I got all of my memory back, would I get all blasé about things like a gorgeous sky, like they didn't matter any more? Or would I remember how important it was?

I didn't think I could ever forget. I really didn't.

I let my head drop against the back of the bench, thinking of Kathy. Of the person I had been. I sort of felt as though I knew her now. And maybe I hated some of the things she had done, but I couldn't hate her. Not ever.

In fact . . . I thought she was pretty OK.

I touched my scar, my fingers lingering across its jagged length. And I knew suddenly that I'd be sorry when it faded. It sounded daft, but it was like the last link I had with Kathy.

Except that wasn't true, was it? Swallowing a crisp, I remembered how the bow had felt in my hands, and I smiled. Maybe I'd take Mum up on her offer after all.

I finished my sandwich and put my hands in my pockets, feeling Cat there, safe and snug. Suddenly I knew that I wouldn't hide him any more. Mum could ask questions if she wanted, and that was OK too.

My fingers touched something square and smooth, and I frowned for a second before I remembered the deck of cards I'd taken with me to Dr Perrin's. I grinned to myself, thinking of Richard. Pulling out the cards, I shuffled them.

'Here,' I said to Tina, holding the deck out to her. 'Pick a card. Any card.'

Acknowledgements

Though I've made some allowances with science in the name of story, my sincere thanks are due to the following experts in the fields of amnesia and brain damage, who generously gave their time to answer my questions:

Dr Hans Markowitsch at the University of Bielefeld, Germany; Professor Michael Oddy of BIRT; and Dr Paul Warren of Parklands Hospital, Basingstoke

Thanks are also due to:

My lovely friend Liz Kessler, for her valuable feedback at every stage. (And thanks again to the EFF, to whom I've never stopped being grateful.)

Siobhan Dowd and Fiona Dunbar – having you just a phone call away keeps me sane.

My husband Peter, whose love and support I depend on.
Thank you, darling.

And Cold Mountain, where the miracle happened.

About the Author

The daughter of a psychiatrist and a drama teacher, Lee Weatherly grew up in Little Rock, Arkansas, USA.

A writer of children's and teenage fiction, she lives with her husband in Hampshire, England, surrounded by teetering mountains of books and CDs.

She runs a small writing consultancy called Flying Frog, as well as a mentoring programme for talented new writers. You can check out Lee's website at:

www.leeweatherly.com

Kat Got Your Tongue is Lee's fourth novel. Her first book, *Child X*, won the Longer Novel category in the 2003 Sheffield Book Award.